One

To Emma,
With my love
to you,
Pete John
xt

Also available by Pete Johnson

I'D RATHER BE FAMOUS

ONE STEP BEYOND

PETE JOHNSON

Teens · Mandarin

This book is dedicated to:-

Jan and Linda Johnson;
Daneen Mowat of 'Bucholie' and Paul Price.
Special thanks to Jo Meller, Liz Salter, Simon Langley,
Roland Willis.

First published in Great Britain 1990
by Teens · Mandarin
an imprint of Mandarin Paperbacks
Michelin House, 81 Fulham Road, London SW3 6RB

Mandarin is an imprint of the Octopus Publishing Group

Copyright © 1990 Pete Johnson

ISBN 0 7497 0171 4

A CIP catalogue record for this title
is available from the British Library

Printed in Great Britain
by Cox & Wyman Ltd, Reading

You're on the edge of something brilliant.
Just one step and you've crossed over to:

Ricardo's Girl

Meet Natasha Haver.

You may have seen her already but not if you arrive at parties after ten o'clock. Her parents insist she's home by ten o'clock every night. And Natasha always is.

Until the day she turns sixteen.

Ricardo's Girl

People only have sex after ten o'clock at night. According to my parents.

So the first time I asked if I could stay out later than ten my parents went a deathly white. And for the rest of the evening they kept scrutinising me and exchanging worried glances. The next day Mum told me how many infectious diseases you can catch having sex.

And the ten o'clock curfew remained. As did my Mum's lifelong campaign to keep my body covered up in long jumpers and dresses down to my ankles. I think my mum always regarded my body as something vaguely disgusting, like farting in public. Even though people had often stopped her to say, 'What a pretty girl Natasha's becoming.'

Mind you, it was only relics my parents' age who paid me compliments. I slipped through school quite unnoticed by any boys. My problem was that though I could look cute – in the revolting way that kittens look cute – I hadn't crossed over into looking sexy *yet*.

And then in July I was sixteen. Time for me to stand up for my rights, I thought. So I tried to explain to my parents how it was nothing short of social suicide for me to keep leaving parties before ten o'clock – and that basically they were ruining my life. I talked for an evening. This was so important to me. But nothing I said could get through to them. They'd built this great, high wall around themselves and wanted to keep me behind the wall with them. Only I don't want to be with them. For I'm not like them. Why can't they see that?

The following night, greatly daring, I stayed out at a party until a quarter to eleven. Then I lost my nerve and ran home. My parents were at the end of the road wringing their hands, telling the neighbours, 'It's just not like her to be late.' And one of the neighbours yelled out to me, 'We were about to call the police for you.' Oh, it was all so awful. I can't tell you. And talk about embarrassing.

Back home there was one almighty row. They shouted, 'While you're in this house we're responsible for you,' and I cried, 'You've got to give me more freedom. You're suffocating me.'

Finally, my mum said, 'I don't know what's got into you tonight, Natasha. I never thought a daughter of mine would behave like this.'

The following night I arrived home an hour late again. This time the house was pitch black, so I crept into the hall where I stumbled into the table and managed to send the flowerpot flying. My parents charged downstairs and there was mud, water and general chaos everywhere.

To make matters worse, the party had been a cruel disappointment. I mean, I hardly knew anyone and people weren't exactly rushing over to me. In fact, that night I was sorely tempted to forget the whole thing and go on being a good girl – until my parents started sniffing me. They said they could smell smoke off me and men's aftershave (I should be so lucky). They assumed I'd knocked into the table because I was drunk and then my dad started examining my arms for drug marks. They got me so mad I vowed I would never come in by ten o'clock again.

And I never have. Of course, my parents have gone on nagging me (night and day). But that's all they can do. For while other parents might lock their kids out if they're late, or even chuck them out, I knew mine could never bring themselves to do that. It'd be too shaming for a start. I mean, what would the neighbours say?

Anyway, tonight I've come in at – a quarter to twelve. A new record. Only I don't feel the least bit victorious. In fact, just thinking about tonight fills me with shame. And yet what happened wasn't my fault. Why do I keep having to tell myself that?

I tiptoe upstairs. I've learnt never to stand on the middle of a stair, for that's where the creaks are. Then I slink into my bedroom. Will my parents come in, or will they wait for the morning? Oh, please let them wait. If they see me now I have a terrible feeling they might suss out what happened tonight. But that's silly. How could they? Certainly not by sniffing me. But I tell you, if ever they did find out, I'd – oh, I don't know what I'd do. I just know I couldn't stand it. They'd be so smug, so self-satisfied. 'We did warn you, Natasha. But you wouldn't listen to us. We . . .' Oh, stop! Even listening to them in my head sets my teeth on edge.

No, I can never tell my parents about tonight. But I'd like to tell you what really happened. Earlier this evening – no – for you to really understand this I'll have to take you back four days, to Monday afternoon. That's when it really started.

I was on my way home from college (I'd joined in September. Another step towards independence. Another let-down) when I spotted a notice in the window of Ricardo's winebar: BAR STAFF REQUIRED. MUST BE OVER EIGHTEEN. ONE MONTH ONLY (Dec 12th – Jan 9th).

I'd been in Ricardo's only once. That was when this guy with a wart on his nose, who made jokes in class no one laughed at, invited me out. And we ended up at Ricardo's. He dived towards the bar to buy me a glass of 'hot red wine' but we left shortly afterwards. My date said he couldn't get within a mile of the bar. But I remember thinking, things happen here. This is where Life is!

And now, suddenly, there's a chance to be in Ricardo's every night, centre stage. I read the notice again. What a shame I was only sixteen. They'd spot that right away, wouldn't they? Or would they? Of course my parents would go ape. Immediately a longing to belong there welled up so strongly that when the door suddenly opened – I shot through.

A plumpish girl with a toothy smile, who introduced herself as Sally, said, 'You're quick, we only put that notice up ten minutes ago. I'll tell Ricardo you're here, but I expect he's already seen you.' Sally pointed to a television just above the bar. Immediately I felt self-conscious. Was Ricardo upstairs studying me now? Funny, I'd never even been sure there was a Ricardo.

I looked around me, trying to appear casual. Ricardo's was much more ordinary-looking than I'd remembered. It was just like a long, narrow pub really; that dark green carpet could have come out of my parents' lounge. Everything was shadowy and subdued, only the bar shone with any life. It was raised up like a small stage and the bottles gleamed like tiny spotlights.

'Hi, I'm Ricardo.' His tone was hyper-casual but his smile said, 'And I'm somebody really important.'

He was the original Mr Slick – and so laid-back you knew it was all an act. He reminded me of a boy posing away in his first expensive suit. Only Ricardo wasn't a boy. He must have been about thirty. He wasn't exactly a pin-up either. His nose was too hooky-looking for a start. And he had strange whispy bits under his eyes. His eyes: they were very dark and surprisingly grave. Monkey's eyes. 'So what's your name, baby?' His accent was an odd mixture of Italian and Californian.

'Natasha.'

'Na-ta-sha,' he repeated, breaking the word up into syllables as if he'd never heard it before.

'How old are you, Natasha?'

'Nineteen,' I said quickly.

He scrunched his eyes up. I held my breath. Then he asked, 'Had any experience of bar work?'

'Bits here and there.'

He nodded. 'Just walk about for me, will you, Natasha. Walk over to the door, will you?'

Feeling rather silly, I started moving towards the door.

'Watch that back, baby,' he called.

I straightened up, and all at once I didn't feel silly. I felt as if I were walking along a catwalk. In fact, in my mind that's what I was doing and I was concentrating so hard on this daydream, I almost forgot about Ricardo until he cried, 'You didn't walk, you glided, Natasha.' His face was one big smile.

My walk must have clinched it. I got the job. The only disappointment was that I wouldn't be behind the bar, not at first, anyhow. I'd just be collecting glasses, emptying ashtrays . . . but still, I was *in*. I'd been invited to join the adults – as an adult!

I tore home to put on my favourite dress. It was grey and made out of cotton. Its sleeves came down just below my elbows and its neckline was round. Its waistline was black and it had a flared skirt which was also grey. And I loved that dress, even before my mum said it was too old for me. Then I put on this bright red lipstick I'd always longed to use but never dared before. Of course, as soon as Mum saw me she was frothing at the mouth.

'What will people think?' she said. 'Going out like that.'

'They can think what they like, it's my body.'

I almost felt as if I were in a film like *Grease*. The good girl who turned wild.

'You look like a prostitute,' cried Mum.

I nearly laughed in her face. If this had been a film I'd have said, 'How many prostitutes do you know, then?' but I couldn't bring myself to say that.

Still, I felt so high and happy, nothing my parents said could hold me back now. I knew that. The princess in that tower had finally escaped her captors. Now the world lay at her feet.

As I walked to Ricardo's I breathed in the smell of the night and shivered with excitement. My parents already belonged to another time. This time Ricardo's was opened by a strikingly attractive girl with blonde spiky hair and piercing blue eyes. She was wearing what looked like an army uniform.

'Hi, I'm Rachel. You must be Natasha. Yeah, I can see why Ricardo's so enthusiastic about you. Anyway, he's about to give you his little pep talk. So he wants you to get changed right away.'

'Get changed. Can't I wear this?'

'Oh, no. Ricardo has his own uniform for all his girls – and just wait till you see it.'

Rachel took me upstairs to the changing room. 'This is the only room where you can escape Ricardo's eyes, although, just to remind us of his eminence, he's left us this.' She pointed at a huge painting on the middle of the wall. 'That's Ricardo when he was a boy, with his mother. And doesn't it just make you want to heave every time you see it.'

'But why's he put it up here?'

'Who knows what goes on in his tiny mind,' said Rachel. 'Basically he's just a funny guy. I mean, who else would design us dresses like this?'

She held up my dress, then started laughing at my face.

'We don't really wear these,' I cried.

'You'd better believe it,' said Rachel.

I gaped down at it again. It was like an ice-skater's dress made from garishly bright curtains.

'When we first wore them, people put their sunglasses on and asked, "Where's the beach party?"'

I held the skirt up against me. 'And it's so short.'

'Yes, it is short. Shorter than any of the others, actually. Hang on, I'll ask the boss about that.'

She returned, smiling grimly. 'His Majesty says yours is shorter because you've got nice legs and they deserve to be shown. Says he took the dress up himself.'

I felt a sudden burst of excitement. I suppose I have got nice legs – just no one's noticed them before.

'He also says he's waiting.'

I scrambled downstairs. Ricardo was standing by the bar, motionless. As I walked past him he sniffed, then nodded approvingly before going over my duties again. He ended by saying, 'I'm going to watch your every move, not because I don't trust you but because I want to help you. For now you are one of Ricardo's girls. I am loyal to my girls. I warn you though, there will be times when you'll really hate me because I will be on at you every moment, won't I, Helen?' He pointed at a very tall girl with long blonde curly hair, a little pouting mouth and large eyebrows.

'Oh no, Ricardo, I could never hate you,' she said.

Rachel, who had joined us now – in her curtain uniform – winked at me. Did that wink mean something was going on between Helen and Ricardo? I certainly noticed Helen saved all her smiles, all her attention for Ricardo. She wasn't exactly off with me, just totally uninterested. As for Sally, the girl I'd met this afternoon, I didn't see her at all.

'Oh, she's consigned to the cloakroom downstairs,' explained Rachel. 'Only perfect beauties are allowed up here.' She was grinning as she spoke but then went on, 'Ricardo can't stand any woman who's fat, or got acne or who's over twenty-five. The laugh is, you wait till you see who comes in here.'

The doors opened. Within minutes customers were ambling in. And they were all middle-aged men with blotchy red faces and wheezy laughs. They were in suits, too, which they probably wore to work. I felt nervous and self-conscious. Then I saw Ricardo pointing at a table. 'No ashtray should ever have more than two cigarettes in it, baby,' he whispered to me. I moved over to the table and straightaway the four guys there all stopped talking and stared at me as if I were a UFO or something.

One guy – he was bald and stumpy with black glasses and looked years older than my dad, caught my eye. I turned away but I could feel his eyes still on me. And even when I stood beside the bar again, he still carried on looking at me.

'Rachel,' I hissed, 'there's an old man who just keeps staring at me.'

She quickly scanned the room. 'Oh, him. Oh yeah, he regularly gets his cheapies in here. He's always telling me he's got a bottle of brandy in his flat, just waiting for me. But don't let him spook you. Look, can I give you a bit of advice?'

'Please.'

'Well, you've got to watch the signals you're giving off. Be friendly but not over-friendly if you know what I mean.'

I nodded, even though I didn't.

'And most important of all – don't ever let your eyes meet a customer's. If you do that, you're going to get hassle all night. I remember once I yawned, caught this guy's eye and . . .'

'Check it out, baby.' Ricardo was pointing at some empty glasses. 'I like my girls to walk around all the time,' he added.

'Slave-driver,' whispered Rachel, adding, 'just watch the eye-contact and you'll be fine.'

I spent the next hour with my head so high in the air I was in danger of cricking my neck. I heard one guy say as I walked past, 'Stuck-up bitch.' Actually, I was terrified and sorely tempted to run away. But then I thought, what am I scared of? I'm scared of men looking at my body. Well then, I'm no better than my parents, am I? No, I've got to stick this out, and learn how to cope with this strange new power I've gained.

There was something exhilarating, too, about the spaced-out looks I glimpsed on men's faces as I walked past. I almost felt as if I were hypnotising them.

If only I didn't feel so gauche and unsure of myself. How I longed to be like Rachel, cool, confident, in control. When a customer leaned across the bar at her and said, 'How's your sex life, Rachel?', she just snapped, 'The usual. Up and down,' and the man laughed. She made all the customers laugh. But for all her comradely jokes Rachel's face rarely betrayed even a smile. Her face was permanently frozen, closed off.

When she saw me she muttered, 'You get the scum of the earth in here. Look at that one, comes in here every night, usually with his flies undone and waits around till closing time, then starts drooling every time we bend over. Many times I've asked Ricardo to ban him but he says, "Oh, he's no trouble and, besides, he's happily married." I said, "If he's so happily married why doesn't he ever bring his wife in here with him?" Ricardo, I could do with a hand here if you can possibly spare Helen for a minute.'

Helen, who'd spent the last hour by Ricardo's side, flounced back to the bar.

'She's playing with fire,' whispered Rachel to me.

Helen stood right at the back of the bar with her arms crossed. She appeared sullen and bored, except when Ricardo looked at her – then she glowed.

By ten o'clock Ricardo's was really filling up. A group

17

of girls sat laughing in one corner but the rest of the customers were men, including one group of boys, glaringly under age. They started shouting and whistling when they saw me. Then one of them called out, 'I bet she bloody goes.'

Instantly Ricardo was standing beside me. 'I will not allow swearing in front of my girls,' he said quietly. 'And if you swear again I shall have to ask you to leave.' Ricardo was quite impressive and though the boys muttered things to themselves, none of them actually argued with him.

Then Ricardo squeezed my arm. 'I'm sorry about that.'

I stared in amazement. I couldn't believe he was making such a big deal out of this.

'I demand respect for my girls,' said Ricardo. 'So if they say anything else, let me know at once.'

For about the nineteenth time that evening I felt like a visitor from Mars. There was just so much going on here I didn't understand, so much I had to learn. But still, in only one evening, I reckoned I'd already left my parents far beyond. How quaint they seemed now. I looked at my watch. A quarter past ten. They'd have downed their cocoa and be winding up alarm clocks, ready for another safe, blinkered day. I thought of them seeing me in this skirt, in this place. They'd die of shock. At least, 'What has happened to our daughter?' they'd gasp. She's growing up and making her own life, that's what.

The following evening began dramatically. Sally was away and Ricardo asked Helen to go downstairs to take her place.

Helen was devastated. 'Me. You want me. But why not her?' she said, nodding in my direction.

'Because I've asked you,' said Ricardo in the same smooth, quietly confident tone he'd used with the under-age swearers yesterday.

'No, no, I won't do it,' she cried.

'Please go downstairs as you were told.' He sounded angry now, and bored.

Suddenly Helen stormed downstairs, stamping her feet as she went. Without another word Ricardo disappeared too.

'Well, I did warn her,' said Rachel. 'I said "Go out for meals with him but don't sleep with him." Still, it's her own fault. I've no sympathy with girls who sleep with men and then say, "But do you love me?"'

'Is that what Helen did?'

Rachel shrugged her shoulders. 'I remember the first day she came in. She was a mess. Ricardo took her upstairs with a mirror and a make-up bag. Then he sent her to a hairdresser and generally took her under his wing. He likes doing that. But now I guess he's got sick of her.' She lowered her voice. 'Ssh, he's coming back and he's got his leather trousers on, too – that means he's on the prowl. Now watch me put him in a good mood.'

As Ricardo entered Rachel rushed over to him. 'Ricardo, I think you've got a piece of fluff on your smart new designer jumper.'

'Oh, where?' he cried, a look of absolute horror on his face.

'There.' She brushed his jumper. 'And a bit on your trousers. Still, it's all gone. Now you're perfect.'

He beamed at her. 'Thank you, Rachel, I'm very grateful. It is nice to have such loyalty from my girls.' Then he squeezed her hand just like he had me yesterday. 'You know, Rachel, I cannot decide which is your best feature. You have such lovely shoulders and yet, your cheekbones . . .' This went on for some time and Rachel keep looking at me and winking until Ricardo said, 'And, Natasha, why don't you come and join us?'

As I walked over to him he said, 'How beautifully Natasha walks, doesn't she, Rachel?'

Rachel nodded.

'She walks like an elegant bird in Persia . . . but then she also has such lovely eyes . . .' He could have been an art connoisseur appreciating a magnificent painting.

I drank in his words and they started dancing around my head, faster and faster.

Later, I was stumbling around the tables, still in something of a daze. I think I overdosed slightly on Ricardo's compliments. I felt light and trance-like . . . perhaps that's why everything seemed to float somewhat that night. Especially the customers.

Four guys all in crisp white shirts and smart suits arrived. I watched them straightening the creases in their trousers while they waited to be served at the bar. Later, I noticed Ricardo hovering round their table.

'They're his favourite kind of customer,' said Rachel. 'Respectable but trendy.'

Ricardo kept sending me over there to collect glasses. And one time when I was over there, I went to pick up a glass when my hand accidentally brushed against this guy's.

'She touched me,' he cried, as if he'd suddenly won the jackpot, 'and I'm never going to wash my hand again.' He laughed and I laughed and for a second, just a second, our eyes met. He wasn't particularly good-looking. In fact, he wasn't good-looking at all, apart from his eyebrows. They were all right.

I didn't fancy him. But I did like the way he smiled at me. And every time I went over to the table after that he tried to make conversation with me. He'd say, 'We've just been talking about music videos. What music do you like?' And I'd give some inane answer like, 'Oh, I enjoy most kinds of music,' and he'd smile as if I'd said something very witty.

The last time I saw him that evening he gave me a card with his phone number on. I thanked him even though

20

I'd no intention of ever ringing him. And I was quite relieved when he left shortly afterwards. For I'd broken the golden rule: I'd made eye-contact with a customer. And I saw what Rachel meant about it causing hassle.

But I thought the whole incident was over until the following evening. I was on my way to work when this blue sports car drew up and a hand shot out of the window.

'You haven't rung me. I'm heartbroken.' It was him again.

I laughed feebly and started walking on. This was mighty embarrassing.

'Hop in, I'll give you a lift,' he said. He was smiling and I smiled back while thinking, you're uglier than I remembered. His face was fatter and he looked older, too. He must be at least thirty-five.

'No, no, it's all right, it's not far. I'll walk, thanks all the same.'

He laughed. 'Oh no, you don't get rid of me that easily. Get in, please!' And he shouted 'please' so loudly that two people coming out of a shop started staring at us. The last thing I wanted was a scene in the street: that much of my parents remained in me. And besides, he was only going to drive me down the road. So I edged in beside him. He leaned over and placed my belt over me. He reeked of expensive aftershave. I coughed, it was suffocating.

'Comfortable?' he asked.

'Oh yes.'

'Liar,' he said, laughing again. And each time he laughed I started to cringe. I don't know why. Then he said, 'Your name's Natasha, isn't it?' I nodded. 'See, I know,' he laughed. 'Do you want to know what my name is?'

'Yes.' Why did I feel I had to keep humouring him?

21

'Promise you won't laugh then. Well, it's Roland. Isn't it awful?'

'No, no, it's quite nice really.'

'Do you really like it?' His voice suddenly became very intense. 'Well then, Natasha, you've given me the courage to ask you what I've been longing to ask you for the past – ' he looked at his watch – 'twenty-one hours. Natasha, will you go out with me?'

I swallowed hard. Oh, why hadn't I followed Rachel's advice? One wrong action and now this.

I deliberately looked away from his face and instead noticed what horrible hands he had – really big and chunky. No, I'd never want to go out with him. But how to tell him?

'Come on, Natasha. I'm rich, got my own business, and very good-looking.' He was still smiling but I could sense growing impatience, too.

'It's very kind of you,' I said, 'but . . .' I faltered. How do you tell someone you're not interested? I don't know. No one tells you these things.

He seized on my hesitation. 'Of course it's very kind of me and that's why you can only say, "Yes". So that's all sorted, then.'

He was trying to push things so fast that I got frightened and blurted out, 'No, no, I don't want to go out with you. Thank you for asking but I'm not interested.'

At once the car screeched to a halt. 'Well, get out of my bloody car then,' he cried, his voice suddenly all high-pitched.

I gaped at him. 'I hope I haven't . . .'

'Get out of my car,' he repeated, almost screaming at me now.

I leapt out of the car and he tore off as if he were in a car-chase scene in *Miami Vice*.

I leant against a wall for a moment, shaking. That scene in his car hadn't been my fault, had it? Perhaps there was a way of turning down dates without hurting people's feelings. I was tempted to ask Rachel, but there wasn't a chance. We were rushed off our feet all night. Especially Rachel. She kept yelling at the customers waving money at her, 'That's not going to get you served any quicker. It's not going into my pocket.'

Sally was back so Helen was behind the bar again, too. Ricardo kept pointing at her, saying things like, 'Woman in red at the end of the bar not being served.'

And she'd mutter, 'Well, that's tough,' her eyes puffy slits of pain.

Tonight, Ricardo's was just a tangled mess of human bodies, arms and legs sticking out here, a cigarette there. It reminded me of the rush hour on the tube. And manoeuvring my way through to the bar with a tray of glasses was like performing a particularly difficult balancing act. A couple of times I got elbowed in the face and once I felt someone running their fingers down my back.

I wanted to go away and hide somewhere, until the crowd thinned out a bit. But there was no hiding-place from Ricardo. I felt him nudge me from behind. 'Check out table to your left.'

I closed my eyes. I didn't want to go into that scrum again. I wanted to run away. But then I thought, I'm being feeble. I can't help it. I've inherited it from my parents. But I'm not like them. Well, prove it.

I thought of Rachel. What would she do now? Then I gulped down my fear and pushed my way through, yelling, 'Mind your backs, I'm coming through,' and it worked. I felt quite pleased with myself as I scooped up the glasses. I glanced around the table – and at once I stopped feeling pleased with myself and stood, paralysed for a moment. For he was there. Roland. Funny, I hadn't seen him come in. It was as if a trap door had suddenly opened and flung him down into his place again. For he'd sat at the same table yesterday and with the same mates. Only this time they were in their causal clothes – blue shirts with white collars, beige trousers – and appeared considerably more drunk than last night.

I was so flustered by his sudden reappearance, that for a moment our eyes met, just like last night. Only tonight, his eyes seemed to be looking somewhere far beyond me. And he didn't smile and make conversation as the others did. He just sat there, breathing heavily, or was it growling?

'You all right?' one of them asked me. For my hand was shaking and the tray started rattling madly. I nodded and turned away. I just wanted to go. And then it happened. Something slimy and cold thrust itself right up my dress. I swallowed a scream, then wheeled round and started punching Roland, tears of rage in my eyes.

'How dare you!' I screamed.

And Roland tried to push me away with his hand – the same hand he had pushed up my dress. Now it was a fist. No, it had always been a fist.

The other guys were smiling faintly. They were embarrassed, not by what Roland had done but by me.

'She's been wanting me to do that all night,' said Roland. Both his hands were clenched into fists. Those chunky hands I'd hated so, were a part of me, now. A chill swept through me. I ran upstairs. I had to get away from him and this feeling that his hands were still all over me.

I tumbled into the changing room. Rachel stared at me in alarm.

'What the hell's happened?' she said.

I swayed forward. I felt dizzy.

I fell on to the chair and Rachel squeezed beside me while I explained in embarrassed gasps what had happened.

'I hope you slapped his face,' she said.

'No, I was just so shocked.'

24

'Well, I'll go down and do it for you.'

She stood up, her tone became business-like. 'First, I'll tell Ricardo and get that guy banned for life. Funny, I've seen him in here a few times and he looked quite respectable. Still, you never can tell. Anyhow, don't worry, I'll tell Ricardo.'

As if on cue Ricardo appeared. 'Rachel, I let you leave the bar for one minute to go to the toilet, not to sit up here smoking . . .' Then he saw me and faltered.

'Ricardo, can I talk to you outside?' said Rachel, pushing him to the door. She closed the door firmly behind her. But I still heard her whisper, 'Ricardo, one of the punters tried to play a tune on Natasha,' while something inside me twisted with shame. It was my fault, wasn't it? I should have kept more distance between us. But I was just being polite and friendly. That's all. I didn't deserve that explosion of anger and hatred, did I? *Did I?*

I paced about the room. Its dull, white walls made me feel as if I were in a cell. It could have been a cell except for the faded purple armchair and that huge portrait of Ricardo and his mother on the wall. For half an hour the only Ricardo I saw was the ten-year-old version with his long lashes and innocent smile, clutching his mother's hand. What was taking so long? Should I go and see? I should. But I was scared. Very scared. And I didn't exactly know why.

Finally my cell door opened. Ricardo loomed in the doorway. I expected him to sit beside me, to comfort me. But he didn't. He just stood there, screwing up his eyes as if he were protecting them from the sun. 'I've spoken to Mr White,' he said.

'Who?'

'Roland White. The gentleman who, er, upset you.'

'You spoke to him first!' I exclaimed. And why had he called him Mr White? Was that to put me in my place?

'I needed to hear both sides,' said Ricardo. 'And Mr

25

White tells a different version to you.' Ricardo's voice was deadpan. He could have been playing an American cop in a TV series interrogating a victim, or was it a suspect?

'What does he say?' My heart was thumping like crazy now.

'He says you've been leading him on. His friends say that, too. They say you had been behaving provocatively all evening.'

'What does that mean?'

'Well, they said when you walk you strut over to him and keep bending over.'

'No, that's all rubbish,' I interrupted. But even as I spoke I felt myself flush guiltily.

'He also says you went for a drive with him.'

'No, well, yes, he gave me a lift but that was only for a few metres . . .' I could feel the guilt creeping into me.

'He does say though that if he caused you any offence he is very sorry. What happened was just – a misunderstanding.'

'A misunderstanding!' I cried. 'No, it wasn't. He – he . . .' I couldn't bear to say it, so instead I said, 'And I don't think any man has the right to touch up a woman, just because he feels like it.'

'No, no, indeed not,' said Ricardo. 'If only there were witnesses.'

'Didn't you see anything?'

'No, I didn't,' said Ricardo quickly. 'The bar was so crowded the only people who saw anything were Mr White's friends and they corroborate his story entirely.'

'So you think I made it all up, do you?' I cried.

'No, no, I trust my girls,' said Ricardo. 'But sometimes, in the heat of the moment, things become confused. That is why I must try and see both sides. Do you understand?'

My cell door opened again. 'Ricardo, can I see you please? It's very urgent.'

'I won't be a minute,' said Ricardo and as they left, Rachel winked at me. What did that mean? Had Roland suddenly developed a conscience and confessed? Or maybe one of his friends had. Whatever happened I was sick of wearing this curtain dress. I threw it into the locker and sank into my beloved grey dress.

Rachel reappeared with a glass of whisky. She motioned me to a chair. She seemed excited, conspiratorial 'Ricardo'll be up any second but I just wanted you to know it's all right, we fixed it. Helen said she saw everything.'

'Helen saw everything?' I breathed a sigh of relief.

'Well, she didn't actually, of course,' said Rachel. 'But I persuaded her. I said I can't tell Ricardo I saw anything, he knows I was up here having a crafty fag. But she can.' She laughed. 'All I can say is we're lucky Ricardo threw her out of bed at three o'clock this morning. Now she'll say anything . . .'

Then she saw my face. I hated the way everything was becoming so twisted.

Rachel shook me. 'No look, Natasha, those guys downstairs were really stitching you up. And Ricardo was letting them because he's afraid if he bans one, they'll all go. But now he's got proof he's got to ban . . . ssh, here he is.'

Rachel jumped up. 'I was just seeing how Natasha was. Drink the whisky now. You've had a very nasty shock, hasn't she, Ricardo?' Ricardo nodded gravely. Then Rachel left and Ricardo's hand lightly skimmed over mine.

'You've been through a lot tonight, haven't you?'

'You believe me now?'

'I always believed you,' he said smoothly. 'But I know you will take this like a woman. And, Natasha, in a way what happened – well, some women would take it as a compliment.'

A compliment! I fought away angry tears.

Ricardo went on, 'I think he's taken a definite shine to you,' but I couldn't really hear him. For a voice inside my head was drowning him out. A voice that shouted, 'She's been wanting me to do that all night.' And then the voice escaped from my head and started bouncing off the walls, growing louder and louder.

'*She's been wanting me to do that all night.*'

No, I hadn't. But if that's true, why do I feel so ashamed, so deeply ashamed? Had I been provocative? No, I was just enjoying being attractive. All right, being fancied. But there's nothing wrong with that, is there? My mum would say there was. But that's why I'm here, to escape from her narrow deforming views. I suddenly saw Ricardo looking at me questioningly. What had he asked me? I didn't know. I didn't care. I just know I couldn't stay here any longer. I made for the door.

'Oh, thank you, Natasha, thank you,' Ricardo called after me.

What was he thanking me for?

He followed me downstairs, still gushing thanks.

I dashed through the bar. It was emptying now, just a few elderly regulars dribbling by the bar. And Rachel. We exchanged wan smiles. And Helen, I think she smiled at me, too. But neither of them came up to me, instead they kept staring anxiously at the door.

As I opened the door Ricardo called, 'And he's banned until you say otherwise,' and before I had time to think what Ricardo meant, there he was, skulking in the doorway.

I shrank back. Then I saw how that made Roland – sorry, Mr White – grow a little and straightened up again. Behind me a haze of henchmen, all with the same fixed gaze.

'I'm sorry if I offended you,' he said. A faint smile congealed on his face.

'Offended me,' I cried. I shook with anger and disgust at him – and me. I couldn't stop the feeling of disgust spreading to me, too. And that made me even angrier, so angry I couldn't speak.

'How are we getting on?' Ricardo was hovering at the door like an eager sales assistant. He wanted this little formality, staged solely for my benefit, to end. Everyone did. Ricardo was quite happy to chuck out boys for swearing but banning customers – real, big-spending customers – that was very different.

I was expected to smile and shake hands now and say, 'Sorry the urge to put your hand right up my dress overcame you. Still, I suppose I'm lucky you took a shine to me. Some girls probably never get groped. Poor deprived things.'

But I didn't say anything else. I suddenly just wanted to leave this scene behind. So I walked out of Ricardo's. No one, to my surprise, followed me. And I walked – well, I can't tell where I went. There was so much going on in my head I couldn't see or hear anything else.

I didn't go back to Ricardo's. In fact, I didn't go out anywhere for nearly two weeks until one day my mum said, 'I think you're really settling down at last.' Her voice was thick with approval. Then my dad joined in, equally approvingly. At this I became so panicky I nearly told them everything about Ricardo's. I really wanted to shake them up, but then I decided that was just too cruel. My parents couldn't take it. They needed protecting from reality now. Perhaps they'd been stunned by something nasty years ago. Who knows why some buds never open? But I mustn't retreat.

That's why I made one last visit to Ricardo's on Christmas Eve. I knew I could never exorcise the memory of what happened, but I had to exorcise the feelings that went with the memory.

It was packed, of course, with people in funny hats,

29

frying their brains with alcohol and roaring with laughter at jokes they'd never heard. Somewhere in there would be Rachel – and Helen. Would Helen still be there? While Ricardo would be standing by the bar seeing everything, well, nearly everything. And Roland, he'd be there, slouched across a chair somewhere, eyeing up the new girl, still trying to snatch what can only be given.

And then I caught a glimpse of the new girl. From the back she looked just like me, same brown hair, same height, same nervous movements. For a moment I even fancied I was watching me again, weaving in and out of the tables, so eager to please, so infatuated with the idea of joining the adults. I watched her until she disappeared.

Then I pushed my way out of Ricardo's. Suddenly eager to move on.

Secret Terror

It had been Clare's worst fear. But she was older now, hadn't even mentioned it for years. It was still there but only around the edges of her life.

One day soon Clare hopes she will wake up and find it's disappeared for ever. But instead, she wakes up to discover her nightmare waiting there for her – and you.

Secret Terror

I've never met you but I know this about you: you're terrified of something. It's no use denying it. Everyone is. My mum, for instance, is terrified of intruders. That's why our doors are decorated with a whole variety of locks and chains. There's even a peep-hole so you can stare at whoever's out there, undetected.

But no lock can stop the intruder I fear. This intruder comes and goes as it pleases. And when it moves, no boards creak under its tread. There's not even the whisper of a sound to alert you where it is.

I can't remember a time when I didn't fear it. But then I was always a very nervous girl. Especially in those years before I went to school. For no one had realised then how short-sighted I was, nor that I was living in a world which was permanently out of focus. It was as if everything was being reflected through one of those distorting mirrors, the ones which twist you into something hideous.

My eyes were as crazy as those mirrors and as treacherous. And then, when I was four, I was suddenly left alone in the house. Mum had been rowing with Dad on the phone (a strange, whispered row) and then she'd rushed out saying, 'I'll only be a minute.'

But she was gone for much longer than that. And I sat in the lounge, cold and tired and afraid. What if Mum didn't come back? What if no one came back? Then I saw something new in the room: a small dark shape, blurred and mysterious. And then, the dark shape ran across the room.

I don't think I'll ever forget the speed with which it ran or its sudden, jerky movements. And before I knew what was happening it was on me, crawling over my feet. I screamed even though the house was empty. And finally my screams were so piercing a neighbour charged in through the back door. Then my mum returned and, a bit later, the doctor came too, because I couldn't stop shivering. He said I was in a state of shock. Well, why wouldn't I be? A lump of dust had turned into a spider.

That was how I overcame all my objections to wearing glasses. I had to know if lurking in the darkest shadows was another spider. At least, armed with my glasses, I could now identify my enemy.

Except when I was in bed at night. One time I saw a spider climbing across my bedroom ceiling. At once I called for my mum. She couldn't see it and said I was letting my imagination run away with me. But she didn't look for very long. And afterwards I thought, what if the spider is still somewhere in my room, nicely camouflaged for now, but later ... later when I'm asleep it could scurry out of the darkness and continue its climb and perhaps even drop off the ceiling – spiders often do that – and on to my bed. And I'd never know. I'd only feel it as it crawled up my neck and on to my face. To wake up and feel its spindly legs scuttling over your face – I can't think of a worse terror.

I remember one evening when I was watching a James Bond film round at a friend's house: the one where a tarantula crawls over Bond and he has to just lie there, sweating like crazy, until the thing moves off him. And I was horror-struck, not at the prospect of the tarantula biting him, but because he had to stay completely still while a giant spider crawled over him.

I just ran out of the house. My friend's mum rang home and unfortunately, my new stepfather answered. And after hearing about this incident, my vile stepfather decided he'd prove to me that spiders can't do any harm. So one evening, just as I was finishing drying the dishes, he suddenly yelled, 'Catch, Clare,' and threw a spider right at me. Even now I can taste the utter panic and terror I felt then. My mum said the spider had never actually landed on me but no one was really sure where it went. It seemed to just disappear. For days, weeks afterwards I'd wake up convinced the spider was still somewhere on my body.

Happily my stepfather left us shortly afterwards and was replaced later by a stepfather I call Roger, who, whenever I sighted a spider, understood that he had to search properly for it everywhere. No, both he and my mum were very sympathetic. Although occasionally I could see them looking at me questioningly. And I knew they were wondering, is she just putting all this on to gain attention? But something, perhaps something in my eyes, always stopped them accusing me of faking.

As I got older, into my teens, my fear of spiders remained. Only now my reaction to the spiders scared me almost as much as the spiders themselves. For I couldn't seem able to control this fear. And I did try.

I sat down and tried to analyse what it was about spiders I hated so much. Was it their very thin legs or squelchly bodies? Or the fact that they were boneless? (I sometimes wonder how I know all this when I've never got that near to one, nor can even bear to look at one.) For some unknown reason it seems to be only spiders that inspire such blind terror in me.

More recently, some friends tried a kind of aversion therapy on me. They kept emphasising the positive side of spiders. They told me how good spiders were at catching flies, for instance. And flies spread diseases, unlike spiders. So really, spiders are protecting us from diseases.

Someone even tried to make me feel sorry for spiders. 'Think,' she said. 'That spider you killed was probably a parent and now his poor baby spiders are fatherless or motherless. Next time you see a spider, think of its children.'

But I knew I could no more think of a spider as a parent, than I could an evil spirit. Yet I pretended to go along with it, for I was becoming more and more ashamed of my fear. And although no one ever said anything, I knew what they were thinking: fancy being scared of spiders at her age! And the fact that this fear never left me made it more and more sinister. Was there some deep, dark reason for it? Freud would probably say it pointed to some kind of sexual hang-up. Or perhaps I was just plain neurotic.

Besides, being scared of spiders was such a girly thing. And I am, I suppose, a semi-feminist. I've certainly always despised women who jump on tables and chairs and scream loudly if they see a mouse. Yet, to other people, I must seem as moronic. That's why I tried to bury my fear away. I stopped talking about it and oddly enough I stopped seeing spiders, too. So everyone gradually forgot about it. Even my mum assumed it had vanished away as childhood fears often do.

Then one evening, shortly after my sixteenth birthday, my mum and Roger went out to a dinner-dance. And they were staying at the hotel overnight so they could both drink and make merry (though they never told me that was the reason). I'd originally planned to have some friends visit but I was still getting over flu, so I said I'd just have a bath and an early night instead.

My mum left me a list of instructions headed by, 'Lock

yourself in and keep the chain on the door'. And before I took my bath I did just that, even checking the locks on the windows. There's something about being in the bath that makes you feel especially vulnerable, isn't there?

Then I went upstairs. I was already a bit drowsy and my head felt heavy. I decided I'd only have a quick bath tonight. But first I'd lie down on my bed for a minute.

When I woke up the room was covered in darkness. It was two o'clock. I'd slept for nearly four hours. And now it felt all stuffy. I had this full throbbing pain in my head. I bet I wouldn't get off to sleep again for ages. So I decided the best thing would be to have my bath now. I wouldn't stay in the bath long, just long enough for that lovely, tired feeling baths always give me to soak in.

I put on my robe, went into the bathroom, switched on the light and put on the wall heater. The bathroom window's made of pebbled glass, so all I could see was the night's darkness, transformed into something strange and distorted. But I could also hear the rain pattering against the glass and the wind whistling tunelessly. A cold, unfriendly night. A night to sleep through.

I bent down just to test the water was hot enough; I hate lukewarm baths. I stretched my hand out and then shrank back in terror.

I'd almost touched it. If I'd put my hand down just a couple of centimetres more I would have touched it. I would have touched the largest black spider I'd ever seen.

For a moment I stood completely still, numb with disbelief. I hadn't seen a spider for months, years. I'd assumed they'd disappeared from my life now, and their terror couldn't reach me anymore. For I was sixteen, an adult. But as I backed out of the bathroom and into my bedroom I felt myself dwindling away into a small, terrified girl again. Had I really just seen a spider? Or was my flu making me hallucinate? For that spider was so

37

huge it could only have jumped out of one of my nightmares. For years it had hidden itself in the darkest corners of my mind just waiting to come back, stronger than ever, to possess me.

No. Stop. I had to try and be rational about this. Just how had the spider got into the bath? I'd always assumed its only way into the bath was through the drainpipe. That's why every morning I'd check the plug was in the bath. I did it without thinking, a kind of reflex act, like locking the front door after you. So it can't have got in that way.

Well then, it must have just dropped into the bath from the window ledge. Unless – I suddenly remembered Mum had had a bath just before she went out. And I'm sure she left a towel hanging over the edge of the bath, something I would never ever do.

Any second it could climb out of that bath again, down the towel and start running – where? Any second it could scuttle under the bathroom door and into my bedroom. Any second. And there was nothing I could do. Unless I got someone to kill it.

I scrambled into my jeans, then immediately hurled them off again. A spider could be lying somewhere in there. They often crawl into clothes. I shook the jeans hard. Then I got dressed again and rushed downstairs. My plan was to charge into the street and call for help. But even as I stared at the chains I heard Mum's voice, 'The world's full of murderers and rapists,' and saw the newspaper articles she was always showing me of girls attacked at night. I swayed backwards.

For a moment I felt as if I was going to pass out. Flu does that to you. It creeps back on you again when you're least expecting it. No, I couldn't go out there. But I could ring someone for help, couldn't I? Like Alison, my best friend. She'd understand. She knows how much I fear spiders. Well, she did.

38

Her phone rang for ages and I was about to put it down when I heard her mother say, 'Yes?'

'Hello,' I said. I didn't know how to begin.

'Who is this? You've woken the whole house up.' Her voice was ice, a block of ice. And I knew I couldn't explain anything to that voice.

However, talking to a voice several degrees below freezing did help me in a way. For as I clicked the phone down, I suddenly had an idea. Something I could do alone. And for the first time that evening I even released a grim smile.

The terror was still there. But I was struggling to the surface of it now. I marched back upstairs and I stood outside the bathroom door. Then I thought, what if the spider's not in the bath any more? What if it's ... I swatted these fears away. There was a good chance the spider was still in the bath. After all, spiders can sit motionless in the same spot for hours. And if it wasn't in the bath any more – well, at least I'd know.

I banged open the bathroom door, the way Mum did years ago when she thought she heard intruders downstairs. And I was about to switch the light on – when I remembered what a mistake that could be. Insects are drawn to the light. And I didn't want the spider suddenly to start moving about. Not now.

I crept towards the bath. It was pitch dark in there, just as if the whole room was held beneath the spider's shadow. And there it was, so nearly camouflaged beneath its giant shadow and so completely still that you'd never know it was there. But I knew. I could almost hear it breathing.

Yet, soon, very soon, this spider will terrify me no longer.

First, I slowly and carefully took the towel off the bath. Next, I switched the hot-water tap full on. The water gushed out fiercely, quickly filling the bath. And all of a sudden the spider was moving. It was trying to scramble out of the bath. Almost instinctively I backed away. But the water was too fast for it. It could only bob along on the side of the bath. And then it started shrinking into a ball, until finally it looked exactly like what I'd first mistaken it for all those years ago – a large speck of dust. It was disappearing now, becoming smaller and smaller. I edged closer to the bath. Were its legs falling off? I think they were. There were little black specks in the bath now, anyway. Afterwards I really would have to clean that bath out.

I turned away. Now I could almost smell the spider's decomposing body. There was a horrible dank smell in here, just as if I were in an old case full of rotting . . . I turned back. I didn't need to look at the spider now. It would be no more than a black speck. I unplugged the water. And now the water will carry it away for ever. I listened to the water gurgling out. Tonight it seemed a friendly, reassuring sound reminding me of bathtimes with warm radiators and Mum calling, 'Now dry yourself properly. You'll get rheumatism if you rush your drying.' How safe I felt then. If only I could go back. If only I wasn't awake now.

I darted a glance at the spider, then I gaped in disbelief. The spider was moving. It started unfurling itself like a tiny ball of wool, growing bigger and bigger. It hadn't drowned at all. Once again it had cheated me. Once again it had won.

It was scuttling about in the bath now, quickly, and confidently, while I raced around the bathroom too, desperately trying to think what to do next. My head felt hot and throbbing. I should be in bed, resting. But how can I rest when this thing is roaming about the house? I looked at my watch. Only half-past two. Hours and hours yet before morning. Oh, what could I do?

40

Suddenly I charged downstairs. I had one last desperate plan. I ran into the kitchen and filled two jugs so full of water I spilt half on the way up the stairs again.

I picked up my first jug and let the water tumble out behind the spider. My idea was that the force of the water would push the spider down the plug hole. And it worked. Partly. The water carried the spider about halfway down the bath. So straightaway I poured the second jugful behind the spider, which was by now tightly curled up in a ball. And the water forced it right up to the hole. One more jugful should send it hurtling down the plughole.

But then I remembered something. In a lot of drains there's a little ledge where spiders sit waiting to come back again. I imagined that spider unfurling itself and then sneaking back into the bathroom again. Once more I started shaking but this time more with anger. I didn't want this fear any more. But I couldn't lose it. Perhaps I'd never lose it.

Yes, I could. Suddenly I flung open the bathroom window, pulled off about half a metre of loo paper and scooped up the spider. I did all this in about ten seconds flat, moving as if I'd been pushed into the wrong speed.

'Hold in there,' I said to myself. 'All you have to do now is throw the thing out of the window.' I took careful aim, holding the paper right by my ear, as I'm not a very good shot, while furiously crunching the paper tighter and tighter. Then I hurled the loo paper right out of the window and watched it plunge on to the back garden like some deformed kite. Tomorrow, no doubt, my stepdad would want to know why there was a roll of toilet paper on the back garden. I found myself smiling. Who cared about that! I was free of it at last. I was free. I even started feeling a bit proud of myself.

Soon I was too exhausted to stay awake very long. I crashed out on the top of my bed and immediately I was asleep and dreaming of a dead bird. I had seen it one morning on the road, lying there all shrivelled up. But that was years ago. I was at primary school. Yet, here it was again. Did nothing ever get lost?

And then I saw something crawling out of the bird's eye . . .

It was such a relief to wake up, even though I was sweating like crazy and I had this strange tickling sensation in my hair.

I was still half asleep, wasn't I, tasting the last moments of my nightmare? How could anything be in my hair? Unless . . . An image flashed through my mind of me holding the loo roll just under my ear, close enough for something to spring on to my face and . . .

And I started to scream. And soon I heard people hammering on the front door calling my name, just like they had all those years before. Only this time they'd never be able to get in. This time no one can help me.

And then I felt a strange tickling sensation creeping down my face.

Rock Against Casuals

He's called Yorga. Well, that's his stage name. And if you live anywhere near him you'll know him. He's been plastered all over the local newspapers. Yorga says, 'Don't believe anything you've read.' Only he — and now you — knows what really happened.

Rock Against Casuals

It was the beginning of June. One warm day followed another and something evil was taking possession of my town. It was like some great virus; each day another person you knew had caught it. And there was no warning. It seemed to strike overnight. But how? Sometimes I'd scare myself by deciding that when people were asleep a strange force crept inside them and started melting away their mind, cell by cell. This was nonsense, of course. But how else to explain these hideous transformations into another thing, a terrible thing, a Casual?

Perhaps you have Casuals in your town, too. Perhaps you've smirked at their clothes: big sports jumpers with crap like '1958 Flying Aviator' or 'Class of 1922 Yale University' on them and tracksuit bottoms and trainers so huge they look more like loaves of bread on their feet . . . They seem like nothing more than typical fashion victims. If only that's all they were.

The definition of a Casual is someone whose mind has been snatched away. A Casual is a zombie (that's not afraid of daylight), a moron and a lager lout. Mentally its brain span is roughly equivalent to that of a locust. But a Casual is more deadly than any of these.

If Casuals live down your road you will soon know about it. You will hear them first: arguing about important matters of the day, like who has the loudest car stereo and who can do the largest wheel spin. Then you'll hear them fighting. At night. And soon you won't be able to find a wall in your town that isn't full of their mental diarrhoea. For they want to leave their ugly mark on every building and every person.

They are a permanent and ever-growing blight on the landscape, leaving nothing behind them but ugliness. I was at a party recently where someone dared to change the music from American rap (Casual music). And straightaway they were on their feet howling, and punching the air with their fists. (Mind you, their tastes change with the wind; they don't really like anything.) This one guy dared to disagree with them. Instantly about twenty-four of them started beating him up for being too lippy. I hadn't the guts to help him. I just left and went into the town centre. I was with this girl. And we sat on a bench, just talking and it was good until those Casuals started swarming around us, scrutinising us as if we were on their property. I walked her home and then I had to go through the town centre again to get to my house. Now, wherever I looked there were small packs of Casuals giving me the evils and shouting abuse and just daring me to take a step nearer them. If I'd so much as turned my head to look at them they'd have been on top of me. So I kept my head right down and walked quickly. I didn't run, though. You've got to keep some dignity!

And the Casual plague just kept on spreading, every day claiming a new victim. There was this guy, Gary, down my road. He was only about ten or eleven. I'd often see him out walking his dog and I'd say a few words to him. He was all right. Only the last time I saw him and said, 'Hello,' he glared at me like I was his worst enemy. And even as he looked at me I could see his face shifting, dissolving into a Casual face. So now they've taken over

Gary. He thought he was being such a hard man. When really, he'd just been cloned.

Clones, that's all Casuals are. They haven't an original thought, let alone an original word between them. But perhaps that's the appeal of being a Casual: become a Casual and you'll never have to think again. Even though I hardly knew Gary it grieved me to see him turning Casual so I said, 'All Casuals ought to be gassed,' which was a pretty dumb thing to say. But Gary was so anxious to get away from me, so desperate not to be seen talking to a non-Casual I don't think he even heard what I said.

Poor Gary. He's just a victim of this brain-dead age. That's why I'm into the sixties. I'm not hippy or anything but I like a lot of the music and the idea of teenagers all being one and taking on everyone else together. Of course, even in the sixties you had your feuds, like the Mods v. Rockers. But Casuals are far deadlier than any of the past crazes because Casuals haven't got any beliefs. Not one. All they've got in common is greed. They want everything and, to their warped minds, that means everyone else having nothing.

Most days I'd see armies of Casuals marching through the town yelling abuse at any males who weren't in their uniform. It seemed nothing could stop them achieving their goal: total domination. That's when I had my idea. I believe nothing in the world is more powerful than music. So the only thing that could possibly shake people out of their Casual stupor was a band. My band! Only we wouldn't be playing the usual 'I've got lovely nipples' kind of songs but real songs about our lives and against Casuals, of course.

Greatly excited now, I posted a notice up on the college board asking for other band members (just like Larry Mullen Jr from U2 did, only he was at school) and by the end of the week four guys all around my age had joined me. I knew them all a little but when we sat round

47

at my house that Friday night, I discovered just how much we had in common. And I thought, I bet there are millions of other people across the country thinking as we do, just waiting for a band to put forward their views. And we would be that band – the band that started the rock against Casuals.

We were so high that night we sat up talking for hours while in the background a Frankenstein film was playing.

'Have you ever wondered why monsters are always roaring about and being angry?' I asked suddenly.

'Because they're ugly,' said someone.

'No,' I said. 'It's because they're all getting hassled.' I pointed at the screen. Frankenstein was sitting in a hut with a blind hermit learning to read and he was so gentle and polite and keen. Yet, what happened? The villagers saw him, yelled, 'Oh no, there's someone different to us in there. We must defend ourselves,' burnt the hut down and hurled the poor monster into a cell. 'It's the nerdy villagers who cause all the trouble,' I said. 'They're early Casuals really.'

In honour of the monster's historic struggle against earlier generations of Casuals we called our band Monster Music and our stage names were all from horror films, too: Herman, Dracula, Carl (the dwarf in *Revenge of Frankenstein*), Phibes (from *The Abominable Dr Phibes*) and my name, Yorga (after Count Yorga but I dropped the Count. Too affected).

Next, we decided to write two songs each. And without being big-headed, one of my songs was the best. It was called 'Turn or Burn' and was about the last man left in a town, now populated entirely by Casuals. The first time we played it together I felt my spine tingle the way you do when you hear something brilliant. (Sorry again, but I'm being honest.) And afterwards when we were sitting round talking I knew we were all thinking the same: this band could become very big. I really wanted us to get

48

famous, although once we'd got our message across we'd vanish, probably to America or Eastern Europe. Most bands hang around far too long and end up singing 'Anarchy in the UK' at the Royal Variety Performance.

But time was running out. And to prevent 'Turn or Burn' coming true we had to get our message out fast. But first we had to make sure we were good enough. So every night for six weeks we practised either at the local Youth Centre or in Herman's garage. I did the vocals even though my singing voice is best compared to that of an ageing walrus. I figured the trick was not so much to sing as speak very fast. And I think I got away with it, largely because our lyrics were clever and the rest of the band – Carl on drums, Phibes on bass, Herman on lead guitar and Dracula on rhythm guitar (very scratchy and loud) – complemented each other perfectly.

Then came our first gig: seven minutes at an all-night festival celebrating new bands. We just did two songs, including 'Turn or Burn', and it wasn't exactly a disaster. Rather it was as if we weren't there at all. We didn't even get any reaction from the Casuals there. They just carried on throwing beer over their heads and having fights, while totally ignoring us. In fact, everyone ignored us. Afterwards Dracula said we needed costumes and what he called 'better stagecraft'.

I was against this. The whole point of our band was to show up Casuals by not dressing up, by keeping things simple. That's why we'd just worn black tie, black shirt and jeans. But then Dracula started wearing a black cloak. Then, so did the rest of the group. Even me.

And that was when we started getting fans, especially among the gothics, who assumed we were a gothic band. We weren't but we couldn't afford to argue. Then Dracula suggested we wear masks. I must admit that really worked. For the first time, at least thirty people gave us their undivided attention.

49

Soon we became quite a regular support band and we had a small but very keen group of followers: some gothics, a few punks and even a few old bikers. The bikers came and spoke to us afterwards and we liked that as we're friendly guys. The bikers totally agreed with the message of our songs. But then, they were alternative people already. What we needed was to reach everyone else. But how? Dracula kept saying we needed publicity and we must hype ourselves up a bit.

Then, on Saturday night, Phibes didn't turn up for band practice at Herman's. This was really unusual. We rang up his mum. She freaked out – he'd left for Herman's over two hours ago. Later, we visited Phibes in hospital.

A group of Casuals had suddenly jumped on Phibes because they hated gothic bands. He needed four stitches for a gash in his neck after one of them hit him with a broken bottle. Well, we were crazed with anger after that. And that's when we decided to make a real bid for the big time. We hired the hall at the Youth Club on Friday nights.

It wasn't cheap, (especially as we had to pay heavy insurance as well) and we could lose, what for us, was a hefty sum of money. But we also thought it was time to make a big splash and let everyone know we were here. So outside the Youth Centre was a large poster: MONSTER MUSIC – JOIN THE ROCK AGAINST CASUALS. We put posters up everywhere. And I thought this is *it*, the night we become big time.

Now Carl knew one of the girls who worked at the Youth Centre, so two and a half weeks before the concert he sauntered in to see how the sales were going. Afterwards he came back and broke the news to us. We'd just made it into double figures.

'This is going to be one almighty flop,' said Phibes.

Dracula had another bombshell. He'd been trying for weeks to get our picture into the local paper. But he'd just had a note back saying the demand for space was very great, blah, blah, blah.

'Basically,' said Dracula, 'we're not pretty enough. Well, I am but you're all ugly gits.'

Two days later Carl checked the ticket sales again. One person had cancelled, so we were in single figures now. With just over two weeks to go things were looking desperate.

That night we finished rehearsing early. We were all a bit dispirited and Carl came round to my house to watch some videos. He was sitting there watching *Frankenstein – The True Story* (excellent film) and doodling. He always carries a sketch pad round with him and can sit sketching for hours. Tonight he'd drawn a picture of King Kong, clutching a Casual in his claws. And the Casual didn't look any too healthy. Underneath Carl had written: 'Keep Britain tidy – wipe out a Casual today.' I thought that was pretty funny but it wasn't until I went out to the kitchen to make some coffee that I suddenly thought those sketches could make brilliant posters and certainly far, far better than the ones we'd put up.

Carl sat up practically all night drawing posters and the more pictures he drew, the crueller they became. The best one I think was of Frankenstein waving a blood-stained Casual in the air, like a trophy, while underneath was written (my idea): 'Kill a Casual, Win a Metro'.

Our posters were sick but we could be as sick as we liked because our pictures weren't real. They were fantasies that also made a satirical point. There was one with a monster savaging this baby that was wearing a black bomber jacket, a football scarf and had a pint of beer in each hand. Underneath we wrote: 'SAVE THE WORLD YEARS OF MISERY – WIPE OUT CASUALS AT BIRTH.' Now no one could take that seriously. It was just *Spitting Image* crossed with *Monty Python*-style humour. A sick joke to expose an even sicker society.

After we'd finished the posters we showed them to the rest of the band. They thought they were brilliant. And we went all over town taking down the tame old ones and putting up our new spectacular ones. And they were so eye-catching, especially the blood on the posters which was a bright garish red. Also Carl had written out the details of the concert in the same red, which I thought was an excellent touch.

After this poster assault we sat back and watched for our ticket sales to rise. Nearly a week later Carl gave us the news. There had been an increase in sales but it was still more of a steady trickle than the avalanche we needed. Perhaps there'd be a last-minute rush. Perhaps. Or perhaps not. There was obviously still a missing ingredient. But what?

Inspiration came to me eight and a half days before the concert. I was idly reading this old music magazine in which some ageing trendy was rubbishing the punk bands of the late 1970s. He said most of them were 'manufactured' and owed their fame entirely to the controversy and moral outrage they generated. And at once I thought, that's what Monster Music needs. Some controversy and moral outrage. But how could we whip them up? And then it hit me. I was so annoyed I hadn't thought of it before. We'd wasted so much time. And without consulting any of the band (there wasn't time) I went ahead and took decisive action.

First I stuffed a tissue down my mouth to ensure I sounded suitably ancient, then I rang the local paper. 'Newsdesk, please,' I said. 'This is Captain Lee here.'

I was put through to a girl with a light, velvety voice. 'Good afternoon, Captain Lee,' she said.

'Good afternoon, my dear,' I replied. 'I have never rung your good paper before but today I feel impelled to do so because of something I have seen.' I paused for a second, just for a bit of dramatic emphasis. To my surprise, I was finding this whole charade oddly exhilarating. 'Do you know, my dear, that our beautiful town is now covered in obscene posters?'

There was an audible click of interest. 'Obscene posters. Where?'

'They're everywhere. The town's covered with them.'

'And what do these obscene posters say, Captain Lee?' She sounded as if she were leaning forward now. I breathed heavily.

'I can barely bring myself to tell a young gal like yourself. They are posters advertising a group who call themselves Monster Music.' I paused again. I wanted to make sure she got the name down right. 'And on these posters this group have displayed some of the most vile and appalling scenes of violence I have ever seen. And I have served in Burma, you know.'

'Could you describe these posters, Captain Lee?'

I began with the one about the baby being attacked by a monster. Nice emotive one there, I thought. I ended up by describing all seven. And then suddenly she asked for my address. That took me so much by surprise that my mind went temporarily blank and I ended up gabbling my own address. But then I added, 'I'd rather you didn't give out my full address, of course. I don't want any of that group coming to see me and give me bother.'

'Oh no, of course not. May I just ask if you are married?'

'Married forty-seven years. Four children, seven wonderful grandchildren and another on the way.'

'Well, thank you, Captain Lee. We'll certainly try and run something this Friday.'

I didn't like that word 'try'. They must run something this Friday. So to consolidate things and also – I admit it – because I was really enjoying myself, I rang up again an hour later. Now I was a 'concerned father of two' with a Brummie accent (the only accent I can do for very long).

I said, 'I don't want my girls exposed to that filth. And I'd certainly never let them go and see this Monster Music, at the Youth Centre on Friday 16 April at 8.00.' This time I gave Carl's address (I was sure he wouldn't mind) and when I rang off the girl said, 'We'll be running a feature this Friday.' She sounded really positive now. I was tempted, very tempted, to ring up a third time. But I decided the paper might suspect if they had too many calls all at once.

On Friday morning I was in the paper shop, skimming through the local rag and there on page seven was the headline: 'Residents Object to Band's Posters'. It was a smallish piece but the name Monster Music was mentioned twice as well as the time and date of the concert.

The band knew about the article but I didn't have time to gauge their reaction as I went away for a long weekend. I arrived home Tuesday morning, tired but happy. I went into the newsagent to get my daily fix of chocolate, when I saw the midweek edition of the local paper being unpacked. And there on the front page was a reproduction of our Monster-destroying-a-Casual-baby poster and beside it a photograph of an oldish-looking woman pulling down one of our posters.

The woman claimed she had been driven to it by the foulness of our pictures: 'I have never removed a poster before,' said Mrs Lanchester, 56. 'But the vileness of these pictures amounts to nothing less than moral pollution. How in this day and age can any responsible person allow a poster which approves the killing of a baby? Isn't society depraved enough without this?'

The article went on: 'Since the Free Press's' story on Friday, our lines have been jammed with complaints about Monster Music posters, continued on page 2.' And there on page two was a roll-call of people, real people,

54

objecting to the posters. While alongside it was the photograph Dracula had sent in weeks ago of the band – and had rejected. Now it was blown up and underneath it were both our stage names and real names and addresses. Last week we didn't exist, now we were plastered across pages one and two.

What really amazed me though were all the complaints. I mean, those posters had been up for a week without apparently sparking off one comment. Yet, as soon as the paper published my fake complaints, they were all ringing up and being outraged. In a way, it was quite spooky, like a kind of mass hypnosis. Nothing's bad until someone in the paper says it is, then everyone thinks it's bad – or wants to get in on the act!

Still, we'd done it. I raced into the canteen at college. All the band was there, surrounded. And when they saw me they all started clapping. Dracula had been rung up yesterday for a quote (which they never used) so everyone in the band had been prepared for the morning's sensation. What we hadn't been prepared for was the rush of people wanting to buy tickets. By the end of the day we'd completely used up our own supply of spare tickets.

I arrived home, elated, until I saw my mum. She waved a copy of the paper at me, the way she used to wave my report card. Menacingly. We don't have the local paper delivered but my nan who lives the other side of town, does. She had seen the article, couldn't believe her grandson was involved and had rung Mum, who was now staring, wild-eyed at me. When my mum is upset she looks rather like a heroin addict. Today she was giving her most convincing impersonation yet.

'That a son of mine could be involved in something like this,' she cried. She made it sound as if she'd discovered I was a member of a Black Magic sect. 'I've already rung your father,' she said, 'and he's leaving work early.'

This was really bad. Dad normally only left work early for funerals.

It's hard enough talking to one parent who's over-reacting, when you have two going crazy, it's practically impossible. Correction – it is impossible. I did try, though. I explained how it was absurd of my dad to use the word 'evil' about the posters because they featured Monsters which are only fantasy figures of horror and used here to highlight the real-life horror and ugliness of Casuals. But all Dad could say was, 'You've upset your mother and your grandmother. Why didn't you give any thought to them?'

To make matters worse, at half-past five a reporter from the local paper turned up and asked Mum if she was Captain Lee's daughter. The reporter was obviously convinced that Captain Lee was hiding upstairs, afraid to be interviewed.

'Will you tell him we promise complete confidentiality. Please, just tell him that,' the reporter pleaded.

By now Mum was hysterical. 'I really feel like I'm going mad,' she said.

I didn't think this was the best time to explain the source of Captain Lee.

The aggro count at home grew throughout the week as the neighbours rushed round to hear the whole story. But it was all worth it, for on Thursday, just as we were having a final rehearsal, Carl burst in late to tell us we had sold out!

Friday night, an hour before the concert, the hall seemed full already. There was a real buzz about the place. Tonight, I was certain, was going to be the real turning-point in our careers. Later in interviews to the NME I would say this was when the Rock against Casuals really started.

And even now, I think we could have been good that night. We'd learnt a hell of a lot since we started and were ready to deliver. But we never had a chance. When I yelled, 'Welcome to the Rock against Casuals,' the booing and abuse started. It never really stopped.

At first I even found that a challenge. We'll turn this audience around, I thought, get them cheering and chanting yet. But it was as if we were performing in a giant vacuum with our sounds totally lost in the noise from the Casuals in the audience.

Then in the middle of 'Turn or Burn' someone threw a bottle at me. It missed me by about an eighth of a centimetre. Then beer glasses started being thrown at the stage. That's when I signalled the band to stop. Next, we leant our guitars on the amps and decided to blast them out with the noise from the feedback. That hideous sound was our comment on the noise they'd made throughout our concert. And for the first time, something we did on stage made an impact on the audience. I drank in their discomfort, then I turned my back on them. We all did. They were too ignorant an audience for us to bother with.

For a moment there I remember feeling quite high. Revenge can be very sweet – but never for very long. And afterwards when we had to be bundled into a black van because there were hundreds of Casuals outside waiting for us a terrible sense of loss took over. Our dreams had been snatched away from us.

The following Tuesday afternoon I was summoned to the Youth Centre for an emergency meeting with their board of governors. The band hadn't exactly said this mess was my fault but the feeling was there, fermenting just below the surface. They were all suddenly busy on Tuesday afternoon so I faced the execution squad, alone.

I wasn't allowed to attend the emergency meeting, of course. I was just told the verdict afterwards, by the

Chairman of the governors. He had eyes like slits, greying sideburns, and an oily smile, more like a leer really, which never left his face. And he didn't so much speak as chant his words while gazing quizzically at me, eyebrows permanently arched. He peered at me the way you might at a particularly slimy worm you discover crawling out of your steak. Then he shook his head.

'So what has been the purpose of it all?'

Beside him was the local paper's latest headline: 'Riot at controversial band's concert'. The article went on to describe us as the 'most hated band in Berkshire'.

'The purpose of the concert,' I said, 'was to speak out against the vandalism and violence in our society caused by a group of ignorant people called Casuals.'

His eyebrows arched so high I wouldn't have been surprised if they had fallen off.

'All you have done,' he said, 'is cause offence to a great many ordinary decent people. If you have a point to make then do so in a calm and orderly way . . .'

'But if we'd done that, no one would have listened.'

'Then it can't have been anything very important.'

'But it was, it is *very important*!' I cried.

Yet even as I was speaking he was preparing to pass sentence. I half-expected him to put on a back cap, the kind they used to wear when they were sentencing someone to death. For not only would Monster Music be banned from appearing at the Youth Centre, we'd also be banned from rehearsing there. He said he'd be writing to other local Youth Centres, too and he said – well, he gabbled on for ages while I just sat there. I wasn't really bothered any more, instead, a strange weariness took me over. Especially when I saw the smug look on his face as I left. He was a Casual, really. I mean, he wasn't wearing the uniform or anything but, like them, he'd given up thinking long ago.

Outside, a taxi was waiting for me. My parents' idea as

I'd received a few phone threats from Casuals. Even those threats were somehow interpreted as my fault. And the taxi-driver looked at me with undisguised hatred. He started muttering something about 'yobs' and 'National Service'. Why couldn't he see I was speaking out against the yob culture? Then suddenly a gang of Casuals sprang out of nowhere and started running after the taxi screaming obscenities and waving knives. And all at once I found myself opening the window and yelling back at them. And I mean, really yelling! The taxi-driver was going crazy but I went on. In fact, long after we'd left them behind I was still yelling my head off like some demented monster.

And that's exactly what I was: a monster, roaring away at the world, because in the end it's the only thing left to do.

That Holiday Feeling

Sarah's packed already. Never has she got ready so quickly. But then this holiday is her first trip into the non-wrinkly zone. For the first time Sarah is free to have the holiday she wants.

That Holiday Feeling

Spain: 7 September

It's six o'clock in the morning when we first see our holiday home – an ugly block of flats. Inside we're greeted by an even uglier caretaker waving a truncheon. He grunts something about the lift being out of order and then shuffles off, without even offering to help us with our (many) bags. As Katie, Annette and myself (Sarah) trudge up this never-ending spiral staircase I remind myself I've waited eighteen years for this, my first parentless holiday.

By about midday (slight exaggeration) we reach our room. In describing it, the word which springs to mind is tiny. There's a tiny kitchen, a tiny bathroom and a bedroom which just manages to squeeze in a dressing table, a chair, two single beds and a sofa-bed.

'I've always wondered what it would be like to live in a dolls house,' says Katie. But at least there is a really splendid balcony, something I've always wanted.

Katie and I pose about on this while Annette claims the first single bed. Katie whispers, 'She might have asked first.'

I immediately tell Katie she can have the other bed. I'm not wild about sleeping on sofas but I just hate it when people make a fuss about unimportant things like that.

As we unpack Katie nudges me. Annette's combs, brushes, even her hairspray – all have labels with 'A' on them. In fact, the only thing she hasn't labelled are her nine tins of bean salad. Annette isn't what you'd call a special friend of mine or Katie's. But Jo had to pull out at the last minute and if it hadn't been for Annette this holiday might not be happening. I must keep reminding myself of that.

Then we make our first trip to the beach. It is already full of spectacularly tanned bodies reclining beneath huge umbrellas. Katie gasps, then looks most distressed.

'What's wrong?' I whisper.

Katie shakes her head, clearly too upset to speak at first. Finally she says in a sad little voice, 'I'm just thinking how slim everyone is.'

Katie has been obsessed with her weight ever since she applied to be a model and was told to come back when she had lost two stone. I keep telling Katie we're not fat, just naturally wide-hipped! But Katie finds all this rampant skinniness so upsetting she insists we all get something to eat. There's a whole streetful of cafés and restaurants. We stop off at the one which advertises 'English Breakfast, just like your mum's'. It's actually much better than my mum's.

Afterwards, to our surprise, Annette offers to pay. She returns, distinctly agitated. 'When that man gave me my change he stroked my hand,' she said.

'This is Spain,' says Katie, 'and that sort of thing happens all the time. I hope.'

Back at the flat we notice two boys on the balcony below us. They're on sunbeds and sleeping so peacefully. Katie just has to throw something at them. She starts flinging wet teabags at the boy she fancies until she scores a direct hit – right on his tummy. He springs up, then sees Katie and blushes and laughs. He tells us his name is Scott and his mate (still sleeping) is Kelvin and they both work out on an oil rig. Then he asks if he can show us round tonight, smiling all the time at Katie. He's got dark curly hair and gypsy-boy kind of looks with eyes that always seem to be laughing. Of course we say, yes, he can.

Just half a mile's walk away from our flat are literally hundreds of clubs and discos and Scott and Kelvin seem to have been to them all. They get us into this very posh club (they know the bouncers on the door) but we don't feel comfortable. Everyone seems to be staring at us. So then we go to their favourite bar, Niven's. This is much friendlier and absolutely crammed with people our age.

Suddenly Katie nudges me. 'That holiday feeling. Can't you feel it coursing through your veins?' And at once I can, for it's highly infectious. I look around me. All this life, all this energy; I'm a part of it now. Without realising it, Katie and I start tapping our feet. Scott and Kelvin take the hint and we go to this glamorous disco, very like one of the big London clubs. Katie and I are soon spinning round each other and generally dancing everyone else off the floor. Every time Katie shakes her blonde hair another fifty guys join the audience. And every so often she'll flash one of her shiny smiles at me just to check I'm enjoying myself, too.

You'd never think that just one week earlier Katie had been deep in depression. Her boyfriend Tony had been unbelievably vile to her and I must admit I was really pleased when she finished with him. Only to my horror, two days before we left, they got back together. But that was very much on impulse and I don't think she's really sure what to do about him. That's why I'm glad she and Scott are getting on so well. Unfortunately though, he's only here for one more day.

Annette sits staring at us with all the joyfulness of someone who's about to be sent to the headmaster's office for a good thrashing. But then Katie bounces over to her and cries, 'Come on, let yourself go,' and pushes her on to the floor. And for a while there Annette really does try and get into the party spirit, even briefly swinging round on Katie's belt. But then she suddenly clutches her throat and rushes outside.

Talk about ectoplasm. She well and truly christened those steps.

'I feel dreadful,' she moans. 'You both swung me round too much.'

We take her back to the flat.

'I feel awful, breaking up the party so early,' she wails.

We assure her through clenched teeth that it's only the first night and it's all right.

8 September

This afternoon is the most embarrassing of my life. I see all these people whooshing down the aqua-slide and think that looks fun – and easy.

All you have to do is hold on to the bar above your head, lift your legs up, then push them forward and get ready for a brilliant sensation. Only I must have done something wrong for right in the middle of the slide I come to a full stop. And I can't push myself down any further. It's a nightmare with everyone whistling and shouting at me to get a move on.

'I can't move, I'm stuck,' I say. In the end I decide to get up and start walking but as soon as I stand up I lose my balance and slip. 'Oh, thank you, God,' I cry as I hurtle down the slide, only to stop just before the end. I finally hit the water, with not so much a mighty splash as an anaemic plop.

Still, I brought much merriment to Katie, Scott and Kelvin.

'I'll pay you five pounds if you do that again,' says Scott.

'Never, never,' I cry.

Then Annette starts telling me what I did wrong. She's been irritating all day. And she and Katie are hardly talking. For Katie, who can be a bit of a villain, has been moving Annette's hairspray and combs on to her part of the dressing table. And Annette's getting so furious about it. Katie says she's teaching Annette not to be selfish. Actually, I don't think Annette is selfish. If you ask if you can borrow her hairspray or something she'll always say yes. It's just, I guess, she likes to keep an eye on everything that's hers.

In the evening Katie and I put all our clothes out on the bed as we just can't decide what to wear.

'You two,' says Annette shaking her head. 'You are funny.'

'She thinks *we're* funny,' exclaims Katie.

'Oh, well,' I say. 'You've got to admit, she's got personality.'

'Yeah, and all of it bad,' says Katie.

Annette isn't unattractive, she's what you call striking-looking. Only, her spiky hair is just too short. And even when she's not talking she has a habit of leaving her small mouth slightly open, giving the impression she's about to start singing. Tonight she also adds about a gallon of black make-up to her face which makes her look like one of the Munsters.

I know she's made this extra effort for Scott who she fancies something rotten. But Scott only has eyes for Katie, looking her usual bewitching self in my red dress. While Kelvin sticks with me. Even though I don't think I'm really his type. I can usually tell straightaway if a boy belongs to that small, highly select band who appreciates my reddish hair, green eyes and general boisterousness.

Not that I'm crazy about Kelvin either. He hasn't got any lips for a start so he looks like a rather rugged member of the Muppets. But still, he's got a dry sense of humour which I like. And he says he's going to tell his mates out on the oil rig about me (he doesn't say what). So it would be a fun evening if it were not for Annette. She goes off in a huff when she sees Scott all round Katie and whenever I ask her to join us she says, 'No, I'm sorry but I just can't get into this holiday, Sarah.'

I don't want Annette to feel left out of things and I keep going over and chatting to her. But she really is becoming a giant pain.

Afterwards we all go back to our flat and when Scott and Kelvin say goodbye, I feel quite sad, even though I've only known them for a day and a half. We exchange addresses, but as soon as they're gone Katie tears them up.

'What's the point?' she says. 'We'll have forgotten who they are next week.' But she looks quite upset as she says it.

9 September

Katie and I spend the afternoon lying on the beach beside the fattest people we can find, rubbing suntan lotion on to each other while discussing Katie's love life. I ask if she's forgiven Tony for being so nasty and ratty with her and add: 'I could never forgive anyone who spat in my face.'

'Oh, he never actually spat in my face,' says Katie quickly. 'He said he had a piece of popcorn in his mouth.'

'I really do believe that,' I mutter.

I do not understand why Katie, who can pull any man she wants, should choose such a miserable dud as Tony. I remind her of one evening we're all laughing together in the pub when Tony comes in snarling, 'Katie, why is it always your laugh I can hear when I'm outside?' End of laughter. End of evening. But Katie says she still cares about Tony and this holiday – despite Scott – she is going to try and stay faithful.

We arrive home at seven, have a snack and a rest, then wake up at ten, refreshed and raring to go.

'This way,' says Katie, 'we can stay out all night.'

Annette has spent the afternoon by the pool and says she is too tired to come back out with us this evening. I'm both concerned and relieved but mainly relieved.

'Do you think she'll be all right?' I ask Katie.

'Oh sure,' she replies. 'She'll have a lovely time checking no one's touched her hand cream and downing a few dozen tins of bean salad!'

We stop off at Niven's, our favourite club. We know quite a few people in there now, and they're all a good laugh. It's run by three brothers from Manchester who look identical. They're a real floor-show, juggling several glasses at once, cracking jokes and even singing but they're also very friendly. They call us 'The London Girls'.

Next we go on to a disco. Katie and I are pretty good at blanking out boys we don't like which, for Katie, means anyone wearing union-jack shorts or lots of tattoos. But still she gets collared for a slow dance by this bloke she calls 'Mr Tonsils' because he keeps trying to stick his tongue down her throat. While my partner is one of those guys who sticks to you. He's got knock-knees and is a terrible dancer. But he won't stop smiling at me and holding my hand and Katie keeps coming up to me and singing, 'I want to hold your hand'.

We're thinking of leaving when this tall, blond guy, who looks so clean-cut you know he spends most of his time in front of a mirror, comes over, grabs Katie and says, 'Excuse me but I want to talk to this woman. We're in love.'

He seems like someone who just loves himself. And I'm not too keen on him. But Katie is. She says, 'He's intriguing and good fun.' She really does have lousy taste in men.

He's called Andrew and he's got a mate called Lee. We're introduced and Lee's quite good-looking in a pimply sort of way but he doesn't fancy me. Like I said, I can always tell right away. Katie wants to invite Andrew and Lee back to our flat until I remind her that Annette will probably be asleep.

'We're on holiday, not at boarding school,' she exclaims and becomes quite cross. But Katie can never stay cross for long and soon she's larking about, even doing her werewolf impression and she hardly ever does that on a first date. So she must really like Andrew.

We promise to meet up on the beach tomorrow morning. Then Katie and I go up to our flat, which is in darkness and sweltering. Annette had closed all the windows, probably because she's terrified of mosquitoes.

'I hate it, all drab like this,' says Katie, flinging open the windows. Then we sit up for hours whispering to each other about all sorts of things but especially Katie's love life – again!

'I was just thinking,' she says. 'If I do stay faithful to Tony this holiday, then go home and break up with him, I'd feel . . .'

'You'd feel as if you'd wasted your holiday,' I interrupt.

'Exactly,' cries Katie. 'Exactly.'

10 September

'I don't know if I should tell you this,' says Lee after Andrew and Katie go off to have a swim, 'but Andrew already has a steady girlfriend.'

Immediately I wonder why he's telling me. I suspect he and Andrew aren't such good friends as they appear.

And when I say, 'Well, there's no point in telling Katie, is there?' Lee seems quite disappointed.

70

Then this evening, something sensational: Annette gets chatted up. Poor girl, she goes bright red with excitement, even if her suitor is short, fat and balding with a maniac smile.

'He looks the kind of person,' says Katie, 'who could suddenly haul an axe out of his trousers.'

'Oh no,' I reply. 'He's just a nice, harmless moron.'

But still, when Annette announces she's taking him back to our flat I feel rather uneasy. So does Katie. And after a decent interval, we go back to the flat with Andrew while Lee, who's been sitting with his arm around another girl all evening, suddenly joins us too.

'Better make a noise,' says Andrew, outside the door. 'Just in case.'

So we all cough, talk and laugh loudly – just in case.

Inside it is dark and silent and hot.

'We know what you're doing,' calls Andrew. 'Come on, get your clothes on.'

Two faces bob round the balcony.

'It's all right, we realised you were there,' he says, with a flash of dentistry. Then he starts laughing as if he's said something really funny.

But Annette is fuming. 'How dare you degrade me by calling things out like that. I'm not that sort of girl, unlike you two.'

We let that pass. Then Annette snaps, 'Come on, Vernon,' and they march out together.

'He's called Vernon,' screams Katie and we all dissolve into giggles until Annette marches back alone.

'Vernon has been assaulted,' she announces, 'and by the caretaker.' They'd just been waiting for the lift when Vernon, growing impatient, started tapping it. All at once the caretaker was upon him, beating him over the head with his truncheon until Vernon fled down the stairs. 'And he didn't even wait for me outside,' wails Annette.

I try to look sympathetic, which is quite difficult when

the three people nearest to you are killing themselves laughing.

After this Annette goes into a sulk and won't even say 'Goodnight.'

About four in the morning I'm woken by a rustling noise. Someone's moving about in our room. I spring out of bed and discover Annette packing.

'What are you doing?' I cry.

'I'm getting the next flight out of here,' she says.

I spend the next hour desperately trying to persuade Annette to stay. I assume Katie is sleeping blissfully through all this until I say to Annette, 'But the holiday won't be the same without you,' to which Katie murmurs, 'No, it'll be better.'

Eventually I persuade Annette not to leave until the morning and I'm just going back to sleep when Katie whispers, 'Do you think Vernon's stopped running yet?'

Then Katie does her loudest, dirtiest laugh and Annette says, 'I'm leaving first thing in the morning.'

11 September

I wake up to discover Annette gone. But she hasn't taken any of her belongings. And I find her quite easily. She's sitting outside the café we went to on the first morning, having another breakfast just like Mum's.

'I don't want to stay here,' she says, 'but I don't want to go home either.'

She then tells me how much she hates it in her house since her mother re-married.

'I just about live in my bedroom now,' she says.

She seems a distinctly pitiful figure this morning and I decide I must cheer her up. Annette says, 'I'd stay if I thought I was achieving anything here. But I'm not, am I?'

'Oh yes, you are,' I reply. 'You're – you're – you're getting a wonderful tan.'

Annette goes on to tell me how much she admires Katie. 'She can be rude,' she says, 'but she's also popular and so funny. I expect that's why you tag after her.'

I bristle at this. 'I don't tag after her,' I say and then decide I've spent enough time cheering Annette up.

I return to the flat to find a note from Katie saying she's going off in a boat somewhere with Andrew and won't be back until this evening. So I end up lying on the beach with Annette right next to me, talking, talking, talking. Some boys come up and pretend to chat us up. Really they're just trying to get us to go to a club this evening. But Annette is completely taken in and to keep her happy we all go to this club. It's very swish in a glittery kind of way and Annette whispers, 'They've even got fans on the ceiling here.' There's also a wet T-shirt competition going on and a determinedly jolly atmosphere everywhere.

But the price of the drinks is appalling, a real rip-off, and we'd leave if Annette wasn't actually enjoying herself with a Spanish guy who can't speak one word of English.

Then a boy bounces over to me. He's like a huge but extremely friendly dog. 'I'm Mark, what's your name?' he asks very casually but his shoulders are shaking.

'I'm Sarah,' I say.

He then starts making a pass but in such a nice, polite way I even help things along. We go through the opening cringey bits of chat about ourselves. He tells me he only arrived in Spain this afternoon but he has been to Spain before, though not this part. Then he asks if I want a drink. We go into the bar and he brings me a very fizzy drink which he calls a local speciality.

'It's quite strong,' he says, 'so you'd better hold your nose before you drink it.'

One sip is enough. It tastes just like petrol (not that I've ever drunk petrol). But Mark knocks his back. 'Lovely stuff,' he says. Two minutes later he's falling on to the tables. At first I think he's messing about. But then he says, 'Doesn't normally get me like this. Only, I haven't eaten all day.' He gets up. 'I'm just going to . . .' He stumbles to the door. 'I won't be a minute,' he gasps. 'Don't go away.'

But twenty minutes pass by and he doesn't return so I decide he must have gone home. He said he lived near here. And I surprise myself by how disappointed I feel.

I return to the disco and it's then I see Mark peering in at the window, his face streaked with blood. I rush outside. He's swaying from side to side.

'Mark, what's happened?'

'I just went outside and these three guys jumped me.'

'Why?'

'I don't know. I've never seen them before but they really laid into me.'

I insist he lets me help him back inside to put some cold water on his cuts. 'Just lean on me,' I say.

And poor Mark's so dazed I don't think he realises I'm taking him into the Ladies.

He sprawls out across the floor of the Ladies while I bathe his wounds. Two girls there also help. Mark is sniffing and I say, 'You're going to be all right, don't cry.'

'I'm not crying,' he says quickly. 'I'm in shock.'

Annette spots Mark and me leaving the Ladies. 'Sarah!' she exclaims. But when she hears what's happened she wants to help too. So we both totter up the road with Mark and even with the two of us he's quite a weight.

'Are we getting anywhere near your apartment yet?' I ask somewhat breathlessly.

Mark looks around. 'Actually I think we could be going in the wrong direction.'

A little later Mark admits he can't remember exactly where he lives. So Annette and I agree that, just for tonight, he can crash out in our flat.

By the time Katie comes back Mark is sleeping peacefully on my sofa-bed. He opens his eyes, just once, then tries to sit up.

74

'It's all right,' I say. 'I brought you to our flat.'

He peers across at me, then says, 'Sarah.'

'That's right.'

He repeats my name, then goes back to sleep again.

12 September

Mark says that when he woke up this morning he hadn't a clue where he was. Then he saw all these beautiful (!) girls walking around in bikinis and thought he must be in Paradise. After saying that we all decide Mark can't leave until he's had toast and coffee.

Then Katie sees this couple lying in each other's arms on the balcony below ours. Katie, being highly romantic, immediately bombards them with water. They both jump in the air as if they've been stung and run inside.

'Oh goody,' cries Katie. 'I think there's going to be a water fight.'

She gets us out on to the balcony and we're all set for a good battle when there's a knock on our door and a voice says, 'Open up, this is the caretaker.'

We all just freeze.

'I know you're in there,' he says. 'A very serious complaint has just been made against you.'

Katie whispers, 'Those toe-rags below must have complained about that little tiny drop of water. Oh well, we just won't answer the door. He'll go away soon.'

But the caretaker doesn't give up so easily and next we hear him knocking on the flat next to ours, asking if he can climb over their balcony on to ours.

'Quick,' I say to Mark. 'You'd better hide under the bed.'

He looks startled. 'Why me?'

'Because,' I say, 'we're not sure if this caretaker attacks girls yet, but we know he attacks boys.'

Mark doesn't need to be told twice. Although once

he's under the bed he does mutter, 'Just give a shout if you need me.'

The three of us go out on to the balcony just as our friendly caretaker is climbing into view, purple with rage.

'Why don't you answer your door?' he roars.

'We didn't hear you. Sorry,' says Katie. Even she's shaking.

He suddenly turns on Annette. 'Have you been throwing water?' he says, his truncheon about a centimetre away from her face.

'I might have been,' says Annette, displaying quite amazing bravery.

'Actually, it was all of us,' I say. We link hands while he glares and snarls at us in Spanish and for a minute I really think he is going to attack us but instead he moans on and on about how he knew we were trouble and if there's one more complaint about us he'll personally throw us into the street.

After he leaves we're just helping Mark out from under the bed when there's another knock on the door.

'Oh, not him again,' cries Katie, pushing Mark back again.

In fact, it's two of Mark's friends who got worried when he didn't come back last night and somehow traced him here.

'Is he about?' they ask.

'Oh yes,' Katie grins. 'You'll find him under the bed.'

We all have lunch together then Mark goes off with his mates but before he leaves he asks if he can take me out for a meal tonight.

'Yes, say yes,' whispers Katie.

I don't need any prompting. For the first time I don't eat off the tourist menu, instead I have Tortilla Espanola which is a thick omelette with potatoes and onions cut into slices. It's certainly different.

Mark keeps asking if I'm enjoying myself and whenever

76

I say anything even the least bit funny he just explodes with laughter. I sense how nervous he is and that makes me like him all the more. He talks about his family – he's got three brothers – and his job in an electrical shop and this band he's just started. And I keep thinking there's something really appealing about you. If only you lived down my road, not in Glasgow. If only tomorrow wasn't my last day.

13 September

'Well, we've nothing to go back for, have we?' says Katie. We're discussing whether we can stay in Spain longer, saying, 'If you will I will,' to each other. But really we know it's hopeless. We've no money for a start. And it's all too sudden, too disorganised.

By the afternoon we're beginning our goodbyes by doing a proper walk round the whole town. We want to go everywere, remember it all. Annette, who's spent far more time going round the shops than us, acts as guide.

She says, 'I didn't think I'd feel sad to be going home but I am.' And I hadn't thought Annette would ever fit in with us but, almost without our noticing it, she has, well, sort of.

Then we meet Mark and Andrew and Andrew's mate, Lee, and we all play mini-golf and then have a great meal together, where Andrew, I must admit, is hilarious. Afterwards, we use up lots of film snapping pictures of, amongst other things, Andrew wrapping his big leather belt around Katie's neck. 'Freud would have a lot to say about those pictures,' says Annette knowingly.

Then we do our last tour of the night spots. As soon as we walk into Niven's, Jim, one of the barmen from Manchester, yells, 'And this song is dedicated to the London girls who've got to go home tomorrow,' (everyone goes aaah), 'and who are welcome back any time.'

The song he puts on is 'Girls Just Want to Have Fun' but you can hardly hear it because there's so much clapping and cheering.

'You've made a lot of friends here,' says Jim.

And then everyone's coming up to give us hugs and cuddles, saying how they're going to miss us. In the end I have to walk away or I'll be in floods of tears. It's funny, I hardly know these people and yet right now I feel closer to them then most of the people I was at school with.

At the disco later Katie comes over and says, 'Mark's just told me he really loves you.' And then I wonder how I can feel so happy and so sad at the same time.

We all decide tonight is too special to sleep through. So after the disco we go and lie on the beach and wait for the sunrise. I worry about Annette feeling left out of things as she hasn't a partner but she seems really high tonight and even recites poetry at us, which adds to the atmosphere even if it is *Ode to Autumn*.

Then Andrew asks Katie to go for a walk with him. I learn afterwards, that's when Andrew tells Katie he has a steady girlfriend at home but he is willing to throw her over for Katie. I babble questions at Katie. 'What are you going to do. What about Tony?'

'Oh, I can't decide anything' says Katie, 'because nothing's real here, is it?' And it's then the sky starts turning a pinky orange. Katie and Andrew dive into the sea for a last mad swim while Mark and I just lie there, watching all the colours of the morning slowly returning.

We dive back to our flat, fling everything into cases – Katie never actually got round to unpacking half of her stuff – shout, 'We love you,' at the caretaker, who frowns hard at us, and run back to the beach where Mark and Andrew are now fast asleep. Then we all walk into the town centre to pick up the coach for seven o'clock. We arrive with just a minute to spare and the coach is already revving furiously.

'I'm going to see you again,' says Mark and hugs me hard. Then he sniffs. 'And I'm not crying,' he adds with a smile. 'I'm in shock.'

Annette bags the back seat of the coach for us while Katie and I totter on together.

'Come on, you'll be all right,' says Katie who's actually in more of a state than me. Our faces glued to the window, we wave and blow kisses until Andrew and Mark slip out of sight. They've taken our holiday with them. There's nothing left but the long journey home now.

Suddenly Katie starts singing 'We're Off to Sunny Spain'. Some of the passengers look round, wondering who's being so embarrassing. But right now who cares about being embarrassing? And Annette and I join in. Soon our voices rise and we start clapping our hands and even tapping our feet, just like we did on that first night, while the tears fall down our faces.

Katie doesn't speak about Andrew on the coach but I notice she puts his address carefully in her handbag. And if Katie had asked me about Mark? Right now, I'd say, 'I'm in love with him.'

No doubt, in years to come, I will look at that last sentence and shake my head or perhaps I'll just smile.

Or maybe . . .

The Hit Squad

They say everything comes to him who waits. And Alex – that's the guy with the black stocking over his head – has waited a long time for this moment. He looks at his watch. Just a few minutes now before it's his time.

The Hit Squad

I insist we wear black stockings over our head. Balaclavas are too ordinary and they can't make your face all misshapen and distorted as if it's being pressed up against tinted glass.

I tell my hit squad, 'You're SAS storm-troopers. You must keep that image in your mind.' I feel it's important to give them the right mentality about today. And as they line up at our headquarters, a set of desks in the school canteen, they look most impressive, a real fighting force.

They're all fourth years. I am the only fifth year. I actually left school three and a half weeks ago after my last GCSE exam. But I've come back for the last day of term. And I've got my water gun with me . . . I only bought it last Saturday and it wasn't cheap either. You're thinking, well, that's a bit kiddish. But I'll tell you, there's nothing kiddish about the real reason I'm here today.

A large group of second and third years are standing around staring at the hit squad. The teachers look distinctly nervous. Funny how they're all going around in twos. With one exception of course.

'Roll up, roll up,' I cry. 'Teachers, make sure the hit squad doesn't get you. Buy an immunity badge now. A bargain at just two pounds and it's all for charity.'

'These *will* guarantee total immunity, won't they?' asks Mrs Mace, looking even more tired than usual.

'The second you put on one of these badges, Mrs Mace, a circle of safety forms all around you, keeping you fully protected.'

Mrs Mace pays up. She's still anxious though, 'You will remember the headmaster said no tomato sauce this year, won't you?'

'And no baked beans and no eggs,' booms Mr Mitchell, already in his faded denim work-coat.

'Just foam that can be removed at once,' says Mrs Mace, 'because if anyone's clothes get ruined you will be held liable . . .'

'Look, trust me, trust me.'

'I wish I had your confidence, Alex. It is Alex Longman in there, isn't it?' asks Mr Mitchell.

'Today I have no name,' I say. 'I'm just a hired assassin.'

'Now, look, Alex, you're a sensible lad, that's why the headmaster allowed you to organise this. And even though you've left us, I know you'll . . . well, just be careful, that's all.'

'Don't worry, sir,' I say, grinning triumphantly. They're getting worried because they've got nothing on me now. I'm free to do exactly what I want . . .

The normal everyday sounds suddenly fade out. Reality's batteries are being blasted into oblivion by . . . There's just a whiff of frost in the air at first. But this is enough to turn everyone around me into statues. As the real reason I am here creeps closer.

Even on the last day of term the same stiff, joyless movements. Mr Stones is surely the only living being to make a clockwork toy seem spontaneous. Only he isn't living, of course. He isn't quite dead either. He's a walking coma with a long thin face, a large nose and eyes that are sinking into the swamp of wrinkles which surround them. His eyes are blank, expressionless, a void beneath a void.

Long before I'd met Stones I'd seen his eyes on a dead snake lying in the middle of a road. I crept nearer and nearer to the snake, fascinated by the strange emptiness of its eyes, until suddenly it pounced and started twisting itself around me, tighter and tighter . . . it took a long time for my screams to wake me up that night.

And then, years later, on my first day at the 'big school', there were those eyes again. They had shot out of my nightmare and landed on Stones' face. My heart was hammering away even before he said, 'Sit down, donkeys,' and I just fell into my chair. After which Stones gave a peculiar, creaking kind of laugh. I looked all around me. Everyone else was standing up.

'So we have a donkey in the class,' said Mr Stones.

Now everyone else was looking down and laughing at me. Then when they sat down I had to stand up, because 'donkeys can't sit down'.

How I got through that lesson I don't know. Yes, I do. It was those ice-cold waves of hatred that surfaced every time Stones ridiculed me. I spent the next two years, until I gave up history at the end of the third year, frozen with hatred. It's what saved me. For every time Stones mocked me and every lesson I did something which aroused his scorn I kept perfectly still, my head bowed slightly, my eyes fixed on the desk vowing one day I will take my revenge.

He is just centimetres away now.

Even on a swelteringly hot day like today he wears his gown. And as he gathers his gown around him he resembles a giant bird getting ready to swoop.

'It is five to nine,' he rumbles. 'All pupils should be in their form rooms – and all staff.'

As always, his voice has all the joy and warmth of a speak-your-weight machine. As always, the crowds part at the sound of it. Even the teachers look cowed. And I wonder, for the millionth time, just why everyone is so respectful to this evil geek.

I step forward. 'Buy an immunity badge, Mr Stones.'

Everyone stops dispersing and even Mr Stones looks slightly, ever so slightly stunned. 'Yours for only two pounds. I'd certainly advise you to buy one.' Then I place the badge in his hand just like those eager street-sellers do.

Mr Stones picks up the badge as if it were a piece of cow dung. Then he starts scrunching the badge up in his hand.

'You're going to be sorry you did that,' I cry, but my voice sounds thin and scratchy as a memory crashes through me. It is of Mr Stones putting red lines through an essay of mine, every page is wiped out and it is so totally unfair, because . . .

I open my mouth to say something that will finally cut him down to size. But the words die somewhere in my throat, strangled by anger and fear. *Fear!*

I am still afraid of him. At this moment I don't know who I hate more – Stones or me.

'Everyone into his classroom now.' Mr Stones' voice is little above a whisper but within seconds everyone has fled. Only the hit squad is left. And one of them says, 'Mr Stones is the only teacher who doesn't need an immunity badge.'

'Oh yes, he does,' I say. 'And I can promise you, before the end of the morning he will be very sorry he did that.'

But before Mr Stones, there are our other 'hits'. Half the pupils in the school seem to have been sponsored for a hit. And each one is planned really carefully. 'No one must see or hear us until we take over the classroom,' I say. 'Remember, surprise is the first element in a successful hit.'

I lead the first attack, racing into the classroom and

immediately pointing my water gun at the teacher's hand. He waves his immunity badge at me. 'Just keep still,' I cry, 'and you'll be all right.' Then the rest of the squad surround our first victim: a guy with ginger hair in the second row.

He gapes at the hideous faces around him and starts laughing nervously. He continues laughing – well, sort of laughing – while we cover him in shaving foam, flour and water. We get a bit over-enthusiastic, I admit that. And by the time we've finished, well, I don't really blame the teacher storming over to the headmaster's office. Or the caretakers' either.

Fortunately for us, the headmaster has been called away to an urgent meeting and won't be back until midday. Well, the caretakers go crazy when they hear that and run after us yelling abuse, which only adds to the excitement, of course. And we're all really high, anyway.

Actually, most teachers do enter into the spirit of things. And after every hit I shoot my water gun up into the air and yell, 'You've helped us raise four hundred pounds for charity this morning.' So at least they know their classroom has been wrecked in a good cause.

By half-past eleven all classrooms have been visited, except one. Stones' classroom exists in a different day, a different year, a different century. Several times I suggest we storm Stones' room and hijack it. I assume that, as the morning goes on, the hit squad will become more confident. Yet, they never become confident enough to tackle Stones. So he remains unchallenged in his time warp.

Then news breaks that a group of third years are starting their own hits. They've already thrown eggs at Mrs Mace so she's made a very hasty exit and we are being blamed for their hits. I blow the third years out for this.

'You've got to stick to the rules. And rule one about hits is they can only be performed by the hit squad.'

I make everyone give me something for the charity fund (even if it's an IOU note). Then just as I am leaving I spot a tampon, a real skinny little one, on Mrs Mace's chair.

'Oh, tacky, tacky,' I say, picking it up. 'If you really want to put this on someone's chair, why not on Stones' . . .' I look around. 'Well, go on. He's not in his classroom yet. One of the hit squad saw him go into the staffroom twenty minutes ago.'

But still no one dares. I can understand why. You somehow feel that Stones is always lurking in his bunker somewhere. So in the end I decide to leave the tampon in his classroom myself, with a message: 'From the hit squad'.

How he must hate the hit squad. And the new trendy headmaster who has allowed it. I bet Stones thinks he should have been made headmaster. He never will now, of course, he's well past it. These thoughts give me pleasure.

But no feelings of pleasure can survive immersion in Mr Stones' mausoleum for long. The blisteringly white walls, empty of everything except their cleanliness, make the room look like a cross between a cell and a fridge. While the desks and chairs wait in such eerily straight lines you doubt they've ever been used. In fact, there are no signs of life here at all except for the smell.

There's a definite stench of the changing-room in here. But then generations of dried sweat is locked in this room. I picture all the thousands of people who've been made miserable here, many before I was born. I'm almost awe-struck. Their unhappiness hangs in the air, a great, seemingly unending pall of misery. Until today.

I stand by Stones' chair. This is where he surveys his kingdom and enforces all its hundreds of rules. You scraped your chair. DETENTION. You tapped your pen. DETENTION. You have your elbows on your desk. DETENTION. You placed a tampon on my chair . . . Just how many detentions will he give for that, I wonder? Or will he just brush the tampon into the bin with the same contemptuous ease that he screwed up my immunity badge. Yes, I can see him doing it. The tampon won't bother him at all.

I pick it up and place it by the blackboard while I look for some chalk. I'll write him an evil message instead. I rub out next period's lesson notes and start writing. But the hit squad is growing restless. They want to move on to the next hit. I look at my watch. Just five minutes before the morning's last lesson. Five minutes before Stones returns. I know what I must do.

And I hear myself saying, 'You go ahead, take the next hit without me. I'm going to wait here for Stones, alone.'

'What are you going to do?' The hit squad cluster around me, fascinated.

'Something I should have done a long time ago,' I say, and showing off a bit now, I start loading my water gun with red capsules. 'When I fire this gun at Stones I'll be splattering his starched white shirt with red dye. It disappears after about a minute or so, just like invisible ink, but, of course, he won't know that. I'm going to obliterate him.

The hit squad is one giant smile as they imagine the scene. Some are very tempted to stay and watch. But I don't want anyone else here, too distracting. Besides, I can psyche myself up better alone.

They leave and I plan what I am going to say to Mr Stones. I think I'll say, 'Stones, this is where you get yours. This is my revenge for so many things. But especially for one day. One day you may have forgotten. But I never will.'

It was when I was in the third year and Stones had set

as homework: 'Comment on the main developments in Elizabeth I's reign 1558–1570.' I spent hours researching that essay. Partly because history was my best subject. But also, much as I hate to admit it, because I was creeping to Stones. I mean, he was a pervy bully and I hated him yet, I also wanted to win him over. I wanted his approval for the sake of my own self-respect. I didn't so much write an essay as an epic: eleven and a half knackering pages.

The following week my essay was returned with a big red line defacing every page. In my haste to swot I'd copied the question down incorrectly. It was from 1558–1590, not 1570. Then I was summoned to the front, sick to the stomach. I crawled before him.

'I'm sorry, sir,' I whimpered.

'What are we going to do with you?' he said.

'I'm sorry, sir,' I repeated.

But Stones was addressing the class not me. 'We have no dunce's cap for you. So I will have to put this on your head.' He picked up the rubbish bin which was always immaculately empty and placed it over my head.

Then suddenly, he started banging an old wooden ruler against the bin. 'Copy questions down correctly. When will you get that into your thick skull?' And he started beating harder and harder while repeating, 'Thick Skull! Thick Skull!' And the harder he pounded, the louder the laughter. The freak show finally over, I staggered back to my seat. The sick had left my stomach and was now flooding my mouth. I crouched in my seat, tasting vomit, while this ringing noise refused to leave my head. I shook my head, then leant forward. Immediately Stones' board rubber flew towards me, scraping my scalp.

'Can't your neck support your head?' said Stones, then he looked around at the class, encouraging them to laugh at his seventeenth-century joke. Then's when I realised I was his punch-bag, his fall guy, his victim for ever and there was nothing I could do to change things. However hard I tried he would only ever have contempt for me. He didn't think I was worthy of his respect, not even the tiny morsels of respect he doled out to everyone else. And he would go on and on humiliating me. I let out a strangled sob. But then anger cut through me like a razor. Anger which led me to do something I had never done before.

I told my form teacher about Stones, certain that he would agree that, while Stones had certain powers, one of the powers he didn't have was to victimise me like this. After I'd finished, my form teacher didn't say anything for a moment, just sat brushing his trousers. Then he said, 'Mr Stones' methods may be a little unconventional but he does get good exam results. And he's been here over thirty years, you know.'

Cue for me to look respectfully amazed. Then he started brushing his trousers again.

In real desperation I told my parents. My mum was slightly concerned about the ringing in my ears but my dad, his brain still in a meeting, rattled on about good discipline not doing anyone any harm and he wished more teachers were like Mr Stones. And besides, didn't I know Mr Stones had been there for over thirty years, a survivor of Olde England.

No one it seemed could see Stones for what he really was: A Gestapo man in Olde England costume. And after my parents there were no further courts of appeal. School was one long pattern of injustice and there was nothing I could do about it. I just had to go on taking every fresh indignity Stones heaped on me.

The only time Stones got what he deserved was at night. As soon as I closed my eyes a stake was thrust into his board rubber (the nearest he had to a heart), sending him hurtling into space on a one-way trip to the sun. I would watch him shrivel away until finally all that was left of him was a pool of stagnant water.

The bell rings, pulling me back to the present. I'll be face to face with Stones any second now.

'Hey, Alex.' There at the door are three of the hit squad. 'We're with you,' they say and file behind me. There is no time to say anything else for in the corridor outside there's the heavy threatening silence I know so well. I hear a faint whirl of Stones' gown and then his familiar words, 'File in, in silence.'

The third years I'd seen earlier enter, heads bowed, then they see us. I wink at them. Tiny smiles are visible. But then Stones enters. I immediately turn my gun on him. The hit squad form a line behind me. He stares at us, twisting his dry, pinched lips. He looks like he is sucking a sweet through an old sock.

'Unless you leave now I will ensure you are all expelled today.'

Threats, empty threats. I want to laugh. I would have done if my hit squad hadn't left so quickly. So I'm a lone sniper. Well, this is the way I wanted it, anyway. Stones watches me, clearly expecting another flight. But he can't intimidate me. I've left this school. Now I'm as much of a ghost as he is.

I look at the class, still standing by their desks. Then I square up to Mr Stones. He's smaller than me. Funny, I never noticed before. Much smaller.

'Remove yourself from my classroom at once,' he snaps.

'Oh, I will leave your crypt soon enough,' I say. 'But first I have a little debt to pay.' I hold my gun to my eye ready to take aim. 'If I was fighting fair I ought to give you a gun too, Mr Stones, but when have you ever believed in fighting fair?'

'If you so much as fire one shot from that gun you are

going to be very sorry. I shall ensure your reference is completely rewritten.'

My reference. I'd never thought of that. And for a second I hold back. But it isn't just what he said, it's the way he said it, so dry, so controlled, so unemotional, as if he knows he will always hold all the cards, world without end, for ever and for ever.

He turns his back on me. 'Class, sit.' Then he sees the beginning of the message I'd written him: 'Stones, you are an evil piece of dog turd.' He immediately unlocks the drawer and takes out his board rubber.

'Your handiwork, I suppose.' He points at the board. 'I think you'd better leave now, Longman, don't you, before you make an even bigger fool of yourself.'

So he knows who I am. I wasn't sure if he'd recognised me at first. But now he's given me his familiar sneer of a smile. He thinks nothing's changed. He thinks I'm still his victim.

That's when I fire my first shot – straight at Stones' beloved board rubber. Stones drops it just as if it had bitten him. He makes to pick it up but leaves it bleeding on to the wooden floor. Instead, his eyes are darting around the room.

'Open your books, 3B. Start reading from the top of page forty-six.' Books are noiselessly opened, then he returns to me. 'I will insist my comments are added to your reference.'

Thanks again. Always threats. A blaze of anger rips through me and I start firing right at him now. At first his white shirt is just splattered with red. But I go on blasting bursts of fire which spread furiously over his shirt, his arms, even his face. He is covered, saturated, it's a massacre. And he's like a creature out of a horror movie, stained with the blood of all his victims. Finally I stop, purged and exulted. There is a stunned silence. The class is delighted but they stare at Stones disbelievingly. If great showers of sparks burst out of him, no one would be surprised.

Suddenly Stones lunges forward. I step back, half expecting him to fall to the floor, extinct at last. But instead he roars, 'How dare you. How dare you. When I tell what you've done to my gown . . .'

And it's then the red ink vanishes like magic. There are small gasps from the third years as if they've just seen a conjuring trick.

But Stones goes on staring at the gown and for a moment there he reminds me of my grandad – that night when he was driving me and my sister home and the car suddenly swerved and went out of control. We ended up down some side street and Grandad looked so bewildered and so afraid and so old . . . Stones' face is a mirror of Grandad's. Only Stones looks even older.

'Have you finished your puerile pranks now?' But Stones has his back to me as he speaks. And there is an edge of uncertainty in his voice I hadn't heard before.

'Copy down these notes on James I,' he tells the class and starts writing on the board. He speaks aloud what he is writing: 'James I came to the throne in 1603 . . .' he goes on speaking aloud but none of what he is saying is going on the board. And I suddenly realise why. He is trying to write with the tampon!!

I crack up at this. And when Stones starts examining the tampon to see why it's not writing, the whole class is in fits.

'Stop this, stop this at once.' Stones is spluttering like a clapped-out washing machine. He is spluttering like a hundred other teachers. And then someone calls out, 'Tampon,' and the laughter starts up again, louder than ever. And it keeps on rising until I fancy it's not just us laughing but the ghosts of all Stones' victims, too.

And the louder we laugh the more Stones shrinks into his blackboard. When the class start chanting, 'Tampon,

94

tampon,' he raises his arm and claws at the air. It's then I realise he's drowning under the weight of all the laughter. And I laugh louder than ever. The laughter doesn't stop until the headmaster, hearing this unfamiliar sound from Stones' room, decides to investigate.

Stones doesn't leave that day. He goes on until Christmas. But this was the day his mask slipped. Things were never quite the same for him after that. There were no more victims, no more warped punishments, no more humiliations. So you could say I liberated his classroom from the dark ages for ever.

I'd destroyed a monster. And yet, when I think of Stones, all I can see now is his face, looking so old and confused and human! And as I see him raising his arm, making that sad, futile gesture, I think, why didn't I stop laughing? Why did I have to go on and on? But you see, when I saw Stones suffering I felt absolutely nothing. It was as if a splinter of ice had lodged itself around my heart. It's still there, so bright, so shiny and so rock-hard that I know it will never melt away.

Touching Greatness

Monday lunchtime in Heffer's Bakery. The queue's right outside the door as usual. And the staff look tired. Especially Allison Wade. She's slower than usual today and looks – well, she looks as if she's had a busy weekend.

Not that anyone asks her, which is a pity. For if they knew what Allison Wade was doing on Saturday afternoon, they'd be amazed.

Touching Greatness

Not many people know about Allison Wade's double life. I expect you know Allison Wade, though. Works in the bakery down Castle Street.

Nice girl. Has a smile for every customer. Never says much, just smiles. A quiet, you might even say mousy girl. And no one ever sees her out in the evenings. I'd assumed she never went out. So it was something of a shock to discover Allison at Marylebone Station one Saturday afternoon. Didn't she spend Saturday afternoon doing odd jobs around the house, for her rather elderly parents or something?

But there she was, wearing a distinctly shabby blue coat – but armed. Apparently, on her day off, she regularly uses Marylebone Station and she's always armed with her . . .

Allison steps off the tube at Piccadilly Circus, then she looks at her watch. Four o'clock exactly. She's got nearly an hour to spare. Allison knows precisely what time to be there. She's got contacts, inside information. But then Allison is a professional. Ought to be. Been doing it long enough, started nine years ago when she was eleven. Never stopped. Couldn't now if she wanted to. An addict and a professional.

Time for a coffee. Might steady her nerves. For make no mistake, this is the big one. The one she's been waiting for. She stares at the dregs in the coffee cup. What if she failed? No, impossible. No trouble about finding her destination. Been there heaps of times. But today was the peak. No doubt about it.

Allison wasn't the first to arrive. Old Andy was there, chewing away at his sandwiches. Allison had some sandwiches, too, four paste ones. Her mum always gave her sandwiches and a can of drink. 'Saves you eating out at London prices,' she said. 'London's so expensive.' But Allison couldn't eat her sandwiches now like she usually did. She was too churned up inside.

Old Andy gave her a nod, the nod of one professional to another. A salute, if you like. Old Andy didn't speak, though. Rarely spoke, never when he was eating. Allison decided to examine her weapons. A nervous habit. Always did it.

First she took out the most important weapon: her pen. Check it, that's the first rule. She tried it out on the back page of her autograph book. Signed her name, bold, blue, brilliant. She liked signing her name. No doubt you'd be amused at her fancy, loop-ridden signature. So unlike Allison Wade.

Now, the hump she'd carried around London disappeared. Quick check action. Is the new film in? Are all the batteries in working order? Bit of a bulky camera to carry around and so noisy. When a Polaroid camera took a picture it was like someone sticking their tongue out. Was it Matthew Kelly who'd said that to her? But anyway, at least with a Polaroid you knew you'd scored, met your target.

Not that she was an expert. Unlike Owen and Taylor, who were leading a small squad of professionals to the stage door. They were all in their uniforms: a suit, any kind of suit provided it's old-fashioned and shabby. A number had their socks outside their trousers. Wasn't compulsory. Camera and autograph books were, though. Vital. Couldn't launch a decent advance without them.

And film books. Winnie, a rare female professional, was the film-book expert. Buried under her trench coat were scores of them. All signed. Winnie liked the stars to sign just above their heads – 'And date it, please'.

Territories were being marked out. Owen and Taylor set out their special camera on a tripod by the kerb. Knew exactly where the car would stop, to the nearest centimetre. Hadn't they got a film of Madonna stepping out of her car and into the theatre, and in slow motion, too?

Allison took up her favourite position, to the left of the stage door. Amateurs plonked themselves right in front of the stage door. Very silly, for just before the star arrived Allison knew they'd be shooed away with, 'Don't block the entrance.' Then you'd lost your place and probably your chance. And that couldn't happen to Allison today. For today, Allison was meeting – in just seven minutes – her star of stars, Ricky Rogers.

Ricky Rogers . . . What female heart doesn't give a little pirouette of joy at the mention of his name? One of Allison's earliest memories was of watching Ricky Rogers in *Good Times*, the American comedy show set in the early 1960s, that ran for nearly ten years. Ricky was the brash but sensitive younger son, always getting hassled by his very posh family and a steady stream of girls. 'Girls, they just follow me around,' he'd say with a bewildered smile. That became his catch phrase. People used to do impressions of him saying that.

And Allison never forgot *Good Times*. Even now, the opening credits were unspooling in her head. First you'd see Ricky at home, bored out of his mind as his parents nagged on and on at him. But then the next shot would be of Ricky escaping from his house, jumping into his flash sports car and putting on his shades. Next the music would swell up as Ricky cruised around in his sports car, grinning broadly and waving at the girls he passed. Then he'd step out of his car, yell, 'Let's go with the good times,' and take off his shades to reveal another pair of shades underneath those. Allison thought wearing two pairs of shades was the very definition of cool. So did everyone else.

That show finally finished and Ricky disappeared for a while. He starred in a cop show that didn't even get shown over here and one or two other things that flopped. But Allison never forgot Ricky. And now he was back, flavour of the month again. *Good Times* had been revived last year on Saturday mornings and became an instant hit. Now it was on early Saturday evenings again. And Allison would watch boys about eleven or twelve – who weren't even born when the show was first transmitted – going, 'Girls, they just follow me around,' and imitating Ricky's bewildered state exactly. And in the bakery only last week this guy had come in and taken off one pair of sunglasses, only to have another pair underneath. And all the girls clapped just like they did on *Good Times*.

Yes, it was all coming back. And as Allison sat and watched *Good Times* with her parents again, just as she had all those years before, she thought, nothing's really changed. Certainly not Ricky, over here for one night to star in two special charity performances of *Grease*, one at 5pm and one at 8pm. Allison bought every paper yesterday just for the pictures of Ricky arriving at Heathrow. They said he was forty-one. Rubbish. He was still seventeen, as those pictures proved: same boyish grin, same jet-black hair, same bubbly sense of fun.

Time check. Two minutes, just two minutes before Ricky arrives. Then, fast footsteps and heavy asthmatic breathing. The last of the professionals were arriving.

Correction, the last two professionals. Wilf and his son Billy. For despite his youthfulness, just eleven years old, Billy was a veteran. None sharper, few more successful. And now they both had a glow, a look of victory about them. They had bagged the big one. No doubt about it. Wilf brandished his trophy.

'Take a look at that, Andy.' He addressed the most senior professional. Posts were temporarily abandoned, eager, acquisitive eyes examined a signed picture, a signed picture of Ricky Rogers, standing by his sports car in a scene from *Good Times*. The picture was at least fifteen years old. The signature though was fresh, newly minted. 'To Wilf, My best wishes, Ricky Rogers.'

Envy shone out of Allison's eyes. Instinctive.

'Caught him at lunchtime, just coming out of the Savoy,' Wilf said and pressed home his advantage by adding, 'Going to get the boy to get one now, so we've got a couple.'

'How did Ricky look?' asked Winnie. That was the main thing.

'Very tanned, very relaxed. Said he's in Edinburgh tomorrow night with *Grease*. Chatted to us quite friendly like.'

If only I'd gone to the Savoy thought Allison. But then Wilf said something which changed her mind. 'He had his new girlfriend with him. A right snooty cow. She gave us this really dirty look. We didn't care. She's not anyone.'

Allison knew Ricky had been married twice and had numerous girlfriends. But it would have ruined everything if her meeting with Ricky had also involved a girlfriend, looking on contemptuously. Not because Allison thought Ricky was going to fall madly in love with her or anything. Those sort of things didn't happen to Allison. But this was her moment with Ricky, probably her only moment – and she didn't want anything to spoil it. No, she hoped

Ricky would have the tact not to greet his British fans with a girlfriend on his arm. She was sure he would.

'He's late,' said Andy, adding sourly, 'They're always late.'

And what a pity Ricky Rogers was not on time. For then he would have missed an invasion of amateurs. They swarmed and squirmed and chattered. All youngish, all going to see *Grease*. All standing in front of the stage door. All moved on by a perspiring gentleman in jeans. All dangerous. They buzzed around Allison. There'd be more of them after the show, that's why Allison knew her only chance was now. Only, all those amateurs could ruin everything. For stars are like animals, they frighten easily. They must be approached confidently and carefully.

Allison had learnt her lesson the hard way. Early days no problem; first autograph, Dustin Hoffman. She'd smiled nervously. He'd smiled, asked her name, said, 'Allison with two l's, eh?' and written: 'To Allison, wishing you my very best. Dustin Hoffman.'

Not that all autographs were that easy. For a while some stars had backed nervously away from Allison. Allison analysed this and decided she looked too keen, too desperate and her smile, such as it was, had a maniac gleam to it. But Allison learnt. She practised in front of the mirror for hours, developing her style: the quiet, friendly smile, not showing many teeth; the deft, confident placing or pushing of the autograph book just below the subject's head, the pen invitingly snuggled in the middle of the book – you must make it as easy as possible for a star. And your voice, that's very important, it must be low and reassuring but clear. A good tip is always to repeat your name twice, then spell it aloud: 'Would you mind? To Allison, yes, Allison with two l's – ALLISON. Thank you so much.' Oh yes, Allison had a good technique now, a masterful technique, refined over ten years and reaching its climax. But where was Ricky Rogers?

Distressingly, more amateurs were bundling into view. Girls in dark glasses, like their idol, and all with bouquets of flowers. Allison frowned. How silly, that just wasted valuable time. Didn't they realise the time for giving flowers was at the end of a performance? These silly amateurs, they were the one stumbling block to Allison's dream coming true. But then a second obstacle appeared: the perspiring man in jeans.

He started yelling at the now sizeable crowd. 'Please, Ricky will be arriving any minute now. But he is very late so he will not be able to sign autographs. He'll try and sign them after the show, the second show. Remember he's doing two performances today, so please don't ask him for autographs now.' He faltered. 'Thank you for your co-operation and could you please keep the entrance clear.'

He stopped. No one moved. No one appeared to be listening. He wasn't a star so he wasn't worthy of their attention. He was like one of those flies that keep dive-bombing into your picnic. A nuisance, but a minor nuisance. One that could easily be swiped away, and would, any minute now.

And suddenly it's now, or almost. As chief look-out, old Andy has sighted Ricky's car. Not that it's difficult to sight: a red sports car moving majestically and slowly, painfully slowly through the riff-raff cars which surround it. Eyes are strained. 'I can see him,' screams an amateur. Several other girls start screaming. And all the amateurs try to penetrate the car's hard shell to spy the pearl inside.

But here's where professionalism shows. Your amateurs, they jump up and down on the touchline, yapping and leaping and pushing each other. So unnecessary. So harmful. The professionals remain still, frozen, not a smile passes their lips (must save those), just the slightest tremor of tension. Nothing more. They are confident that their positions are the right ones. They can score a direct hit here. No problem. If only the amateurs don't block their target area.

The car stops. A door opens and life plunges into fast-forward. A minute, that's all the scene lasts for. Two anonymous-looking men get out of the car and one opens the door for a star in a white T-shirt, black jacket and black jeans, who bounds out of the car exactly as he did at the beginning of every episode of *Good Times* and waves at the crowd, then he sees some flowers walking towards him, takes them, says, 'You're brilliant,' gives the flowers to one of the anonymous-looking men and then says, 'I'm sorry,' four times to autograph hunters. The man in jeans is shrieking at the crowd now: 'Come on, leave a gangway for Ricky like I said.' Shortly afterwards a surge of fans knocks him over. He doesn't say anything else. But just a wave and a grin from Ricky and the crowd part. People call out, 'Give us a kiss, Ricky', and 'Ricky, I love you', and 'Girls still follow you about, Ricky', and so many pictures of him are waved in the air it is like a Ricky Rogers' flag day. Then he gives one last wave, cries, 'Let's go with the good times,' which sets off more screaming and then he's gone.

It's a blur, a disappointing blur. Except for one person. For one person it's a moment that's already being replayed. For just as Ricky reached the stage door, the time when stars feel at their most secure, an autograph book was splayed in front of him, pen all ready, page clean and waiting. And a girl, not exactly pretty but with a gentle, friendly smile asked so politely, 'Would you mind? To Allison. With two l's. Yes, Allison. ALLISON. Thank you so much.' Then she added, 'Welcome to England, Ricky,' as she snapped a picture of him.

'Thank you, Allison, I'm really pleased to be here,' he said and in her book he'd scrawled: 'Dear Allison. With love, Ricky Rogers.'

Only autograph he'd signed.

Did that scene last fifteen seconds? Just. But in that time she had stood face to face with Ricky. (He was smaller than she'd imagined – no more than 5'7" – they usually are smaller, of course.) She'd spoken to Ricky, thanked Ricky, oh, yes and she had touched Ricky, very lightly, when she took back the autograph book. And then he smiled at her. At her! And the moment was quite undiluted by any of his girlfriends. But then Allison knew Ricky had too much taste to bring along girlfriends to an occasion like this.

The amateurs pour round to the front of the theatre, off to see the show. But for the professionals the show's over. Disappointed, certainly. Wilf cuffs Billy over the head. For Billy had him. Lured over by the bait of youth, Ricky was about to sign.

But: 'First rule, check your pen is full,' snarls Wilf.

'It was,' wails Billy. 'Must have been the way he held it.'

'Far too many people here. Blocked our view entirely,' moans Owen as he and Taylor dismantle their equipment. 'He should have sat on the car like Gary Glitter did.'

No, not a vintage haul. But they were professionals and Winnie is already rifling through her books for her nice picture of Timothy Dalton. He's the next stop at the Queen's Theatre. The show must go on.

Allison isn't going to the show either. She doesn't want to see Ricky in *Grease*, it would only distort her memories of him in *Good Times*. But she doesn't go off with them to the Queen's Theatre either. She wants a moment to let it all sink in. She goes round to the front of the theatre. There are pictures of Ricky Rogers, helping her absorb the full glory of her achievement. Must recall it totally so that one cold, grey Monday morning when she's assaulted by tedium, she can call up the moment she touched greatness.

She takes the autograph book out again. Just one more

look. She gazes at his autograph wonderingly. She still can't believe it. Then gently, tenderly, she puts it away. When she gets home tonight she will stick her Polaroid picture of Ricky beside it, just to set it off.

The audience are piling into the theatre now. Allison gives them a sad, pitying look. None of them will ever get nearer to Ricky Rogers than the front row of the stalls. Still, they seem content with that.

Strange, how people can be happy with so little.

Letter from a Vaporised Sixteen-year-old

Jason doesn't write letters. He just can't find the time for a start. Until tonight. Over and over he's written this letter in his head. Until finally . . .

Letter from a Vaporised Sixteen-year-old

7 April

Dear Kara,

At the moment it is twenty to four in the early hours of Sunday morning. And I've decided to write to you as a change from thinking about you. I also thought you might be feeling just the tiniest bit guilty about blanking me out tonight. At the time, I admit, it was a bit of a shocker but now, after mature reflection and a few illicit glasses of my dad's home-made wine, I think you were quite right.

It's a weird sensation though, having someone look right through you as if you're not there. I've always wondered what it would be like to be invisible and now I know. Thank you for adding to my experiences of life.

While I'm thanking you – thanks for the two best weeks of my life. To think, my mates and I only went to that party to annoy its host, Fatty Hair-Bear. But then I saw a really tall, beautiful girl with a fantastic smile – that's you, in case you're too modest to recognise yourself. And I went up to you and tried to appear as friendly and witty as possible. Then I said, 'I'm Jason,' and you said, 'Hi-i-i-i, Jason,' in a way that made my hair curl with excitement. (I've got very excitable hair.) I can't remember when you told me your name. Perhaps I always knew it.

Next we danced together and I thought I was really

impressing you until one of my mates asked if I was dancing like that for a bet.

You must admit I was a sparkling conversationalist though, with dazzling questions like, 'Where have you come from?' Still, you couldn't just say that you lived two doors away from Fatty Hair-Bear and had just broken up from your very elite private school. Could you? Instead you said, 'I'm on the run – from a travel agent.' Then you told me the story of the travel agent who booked you and your mum a holiday in Portugal, followed you there and pestered you so much you ended up leaving your holiday two days early.

You were always talking about your holiday romances. In fact, you can't walk into a bar without a guy appearing and hissing, 'Come back at midnight, beautiful lady.' Can you? Are you seeing someone now? Don't answer that question. Even an invisible man has feelings.

Still, after that party *you* chased me. Well, you rang me up and suggested I take you out for a meal. You even recommended the place, Circos, probably the most expensive restaurant known to Western civilisation. I used up most of my savings that night, you know. But fear not, gentle Kara, you were worth it.

Even though you thought I let you down by not wearing a suit. Go on, you can admit it. Actually, I have got a suit. It lurks in the very back of my wardrobe. My interview suit I call it – no wonder I never get any jobs! But perhaps when I'm twenty-one and boring, I'll happily ponce around in suits all the time. But right now suits are alien to me, while my leather jacket is part of my life, my ethics, it is me. Even though wearing it means I have to smile eight times brighter than anyone else, so they won't automatically judge me. And I have to put up with waiters giving me patronising looks, though I'm probably more cultured than they are.

I also had to put up with you at the end of the meal

saying, 'I'd offer you a lift but if Daddy sees you dressed like that he'll think I've been out with a right hoodlum, which I have,' you added with a merry laugh. I laughed, too, but I was burning up inside.

Still, I ended the evening in true hoodlum style, didn't I? Just think, while we were laughing inside Circos, Fatty Hair-Bear's gang was outside plotting my destruction. If only I'd spotted them. IF ONLY.

But (sob) I didn't and seconds after you and Daddy left they kicked the hell out of me. Took seven of them to do it, though. EGO STRIKES AGAIN! Then they raced into their cars and left me coughing up my guts and most of my blood supply. And I'm not writing this in a desperate bid for your sympathy (yes I am), but to show you that what happened wasn't just a scuffle which got out of hand, as you rather annoyingly kept describing it. (Some scuffle – seven to one.) Fatty Hair-Bear's gang was wild with anger that a girl from their territory would go out with one of the low life off the estate. They were punishing me and warning me off.

Years ago I was in a gang, or firm as we quaintly termed ourselves, and we used to have mass-fights with the posh prats from Fatty Hair-Bear's road. But that was practically before time began and though I would still list annoying Fatty Hair-Bear as one of my favourite leisure pursuits, I gave up having fights with his gang about the same time I gave up marbles. Or so I'd thought.

Back to that night. I was lying in the gutter, thinking I've definitely had better nights than this, when along comes Headcase Steve. He was in my old gang (I say my gang, though it wasn't *my* gang. Confused?) and if he and Danny hadn't taken me home that night, I might really be invisible now.

So then, I was ill in bed, having many visitors because I'm a popular guy (ha, ha), and one very special one. It was in the afternoon. I'd been drifting in and out of sleep and suddenly, there you were, in my bedroom. And the way you smiled at me – no one's smiled at me like that since I was four and visited Father Christmas in his grotto. Of course you didn't have a beard but otherwise you were a dead ringer for him. Relation of yours, perhaps?

Which reminds me – your parents. I'll never forget the first time I went round your house. You rushed upstairs, leaving me in your front room with your mother and brother Alan, who was watching this sports quiz. Only that was switched off the second I came in and your mum sat smiling at me. Then your dad suddenly appeared, too. And both your parents were very genial, in the way people conducting interviews are genial. They were relaxing me to suss out my prospects. Even when your dad and I were playing pool (and I let him win) the interview went on.

I failed it, of course. Doing GCSE resits, living on that awful council estate and wearing a leather jacket. I could feel the trap door opening up beneath me. A definite pleb, throw him down to the crocodiles! Only your parents weren't that savage. In fact they were very nice to me. Probably because they figured I was just a phase. 'Poor Kara, she's going through her bit-of-rough phase. Oh well, it won't last long. Shudder! Shudder.'

And I wanted to fit into your house so badly. That's why I even asked you what clothes I should wear. You replied, 'Just wear whatever you feel comfortable in. Don't worry about my parents,' which was great. The following day you bought me that white shirt and tie. And when I wore it you said, 'Oh you look so much better in smart clothes,' and offered to help me to buy some new trousers.

So there I was in my white shirt and new trousers, every night, until Thursday 28 March. That night it was back to the ripped jeans again . . . I didn't tell you why, because I didn't want you to have to get involved. This is

114

where Kara laughs sarcastically. But it's true, so stop laughing sarcastically and let me tell you what happened. My gang had set a trap for Fatty Hair-Bear that night. You were only involved because Fatty Hair-Bear was watching your house. I was meant to leave your house early but there was this terrible thunderstorm and you said, 'I don't mind the thunder, it's the lightning which spooks me.' And every time the gap between the thunder and lightning seemed to get shorter. Until, finally, there was no gap at all and the lightning lit up the house and you were shaking in my arms. Or was it me shaking in your arms?

Afterwards you looked quite concerned when I refused a lift home from your dad. 'Is it safe on your own?' you asked, like you *really cared*. I was mighty tempted then to forget the whole thing and have a lift from your dad after all. If I had we'd – but I didn't. And my reason was such a noble one you'll want to heave up. So get ready.

I COULDN'T LET MY MATES DOWN. Pause for Kara to throw up. But think about it. My old gang had rejoined for me. They'd plotted this revenge ambush *for me*. So I couldn't run out on them, could I?

Anyway, I made a noisy exit from your house and of course Fatty Hair-Bear and a few of his gang started trailing me. I pretended (!) to be scared and began to run, knowing this would really give them a taste for some blood-letting. Sure enough, they started racing after me . . . then yelling insults in their posh voices. They sounded quite funny actually, especially as some of their voices hadn't broken yet. And then my gang came roaring on to the scene. And there was one almighty scrum.

I hate violence, Kara. Partly (mainly) because I'm a lifelong coward but also because I know it's senseless. And it *disturbs* me. And yet that fight felt different. For this was all of us fighting together. And I could actually feel the energy of everybody who was there fighting for

115

me. And even though I got hit on the nose, jaw and eye. I really didn't feel a thing. I was that high.

And after we'd defeated Fatty Hair-Bear's rejects we marched back to our estate, victorious. I tell you Kara, it was like the last scene of a film. I could almost hear the music swelling up behind us. Then we went and sat on this wall by the mill, where we used to sit in ye olden days. And it was like we'd gone back to the past for one last, sensational firm-up. And we'd totally wiped Fatty Hair-Bear out this time.

Then the gang wanted to meet you. So I arranged that, just before we went to the pictures, we'd meet them in McDonald's. You see, I was proud of you and I wanted to show you off.

And right now I need a cough and a drink. So there will be a short interval.

I nearly didn't come back. For I've reached 29 March. But I guess there's no way round it. And I want to give you my side of that night, even though I probably won't post this letter.

So, it's eight o'clock on 29 March. And you're meeting my mates. You weren't very keen to meet them but you did it for me. And you quickly won them over. You can be a real charmer when you want. And we were about to leave for the pictures when suddenly the Fatty Hair-Bear Choral Society started up. They can only remember one word per evening. And that night SLAG was the word.

At first you didn't realise this chant was dedicated to you. Why should you? And when you did – you valiantly tried to laugh it off. I really admired you then. For it must have been a shock, especially as you'd always got on with Fatty Hair-Bear and had no idea he thought you'd set him up.

This chanting got louder and louder until Headcase

116

Steve said, 'We're not taking this, are we?' and threw his food down and steamed outside. That's when you looked at me and for a split second there, if I'd acted quickly, maybe I could have stopped him. But – I didn't.

Instead I followed Headcase Steve outside. And watched Fatty Hair-Bear's Choral Society quickly disband. Headcase Steve was not to be messed with. And anyway they'd achieved their goal: destroyed our evening.

But one boy didn't leg it quickly enough. And Steve lunged at him. But I swear to you, Steve would never have pulled a knife on the boy. He hardly ever used knives. And he wouldn't have then, if this other guy hadn't tried to take Steve from behind. A crazy thing to do. And that's when Steve whipped round and, in a blinding frenzy, stabbed the guy, who immediately fell to the ground. But it's Steve I'm seeing now, standing there with blood all over his coat and a puzzled expression on his face.

He looked across at me but it was as if my mind had suddenly jammed up. Then you screamed and Steve threw his knife into the fountain and ran, while people appeared from everywhere. And you were shaking. I went to put my arm around you but you turned on me, yelling, 'Your friends are monsters,' and that made me angry. It still does to be honest, because I know Steve. And he isn't a monster.

He's a seventeen-year-old guy with a bashed-up nose who's going bald. He was in the bottom stream for everything and won't be carrying away any sporting medals this century. He'd be dismissed with a sneer as Bald Steve if it weren't for one thing . . . he was the hardest guy in my year, probably in the school. As well as Headcase Steve he's known as Burnt-out Robot because when he fights he just goes mad and never stops.

That's what gained him all his respect – and will put him away for two years.

The same day I saw Steve in the remand centre I visited Mark, the guy Steve knifed. To my surprise we talked for over an hour. We'd played football together years ago. I'd totally forgotten but he hadn't. He's going to be all right, by the way.

Then afterwards I sat on the wall by the mill, thinking about a lot of things but especially about all the time we spend trying to show people we're not who we are. It's as if we're ashamed of our real selves, so we've always got to be putting on disguises.

Like, after the knifing, I was really shaken up. The sweat was just pouring down my back but still I felt I had to look cool, unfazed. That's why when you cried, 'I don't want to be pulled into this,' I was highly embarrassed. I thought, Kara's blowing my cover. Especially as everyone was watching us (or so it seemed to me). So I let you jump into that taxi and I didn't follow you. Since then, I've run that scene over and over in my head. And every time I've jumped into that taxi with you. But that doesn't count, that doesn't alter a thing. They're just like all those apologies I've made to you in my head – you can't hear them, can you?

And there's no way I can make you hear me. For you're never in when I ring, though I know you are really. And then tonight, you just looked right through me. Proof positive your memory-banks are now wiped clean of Jason Howe and I have been well and truly vaporised. But, like I wrote at the beginning, I don't blame you. I just think you might have given me a chance to explain and say, I'm *TRULY, TRULY, SORRY*.

It's getting light now. A new day dawns. The day Kara reads this letter. For I'm going to deliver it personally to your house, right now. But before I sign off, being vaporised does have its perks, you know. Well, one perk.

118

It means you can say the things you've always wanted to say but never dared, because normally I just can't say things like that. Now I can but all the words I want to use seem worn out, they're like records that have been played so often all you can hear now are the scratches. Unless you listen very carefully, then you might just hear: I'll love you for ever.

Jason
XXX

P.S. Always glad to hear from you.

... And his Vaporiser Replies

Thursday 11 April

Dear Jason,

I've only just received your letter, for reasons I'll explain later. I'm writing back immediately.

I never vaporised you. You vaporised yourself that night, standing there with the rest of your gang, all with identical mask expressions on your faces and on that mask was everything I hated. And your mask never slipped that night, not even when that poor guy got knifed for trying to help his friend. I actually saw that knife go into him. And I'll never forget that. Nor the sight of him just lying there with his hands over his head. It could so easily have been you killed – and for what?

You say you were shaken up by what you saw but even in your letter you show sympathy for his potential murderer. Personally, I'd put him away for a lot longer than two years.

And you say you thought I'd blown your cover. It showed. Even when I ran into that taxi – and I was hoping you'd at least try and comfort me – you just gave me a really cold stare. And I thought, who is this guy? And what am I doing going out with him? I didn't know you any more.

Or perhaps, I'd never *really* known you. When we met our lives just instantly ran into each other. Or so it seemed. After meeting you at that party I couldn't imagine a day without you.

Jason, those two weeks were very special for me, too. I'll never lose them. How could I? And yet, it was just two weeks we'd had together, about the length of one of my holiday romances. I haven't had as many holiday romances as you seem to think but there have been some. Partly because my parents are always jetting off somewhere. And holiday romances suit me because they're very short, very sweet and never go beyond Phase One. You know Phase One, that's when you meet someone and think he's wonderful. Phase Two is when you discover the truth. That's why, once the holiday is over, I never even pretend I'm going to see him again. He's an illusion, a wonderful illusion but he can't survive reality. No one can.

For two weeks you were the most wonderful illusion of all. Every day you'd do something. It might be just a very small thing – like, do you remember when we were playing tennis and I didn't have any socks on, yet the second I said my shoes were rubbing against my feet you whipped off your socks – you didn't even have to think about it – and gave them to me? They were pretty sweaty actually but it was a beautiful gesture.

Just think, if we'd parted on the 28th we'd only have good memories of each other now. Instead of which, we lingered too long and dropped into Phase Two. That's why after the taxi dropped me home I wrote you a letter saying I thought it would be better if we finished.

I've written you so many letters. My bin now has quite a collection of these unfinished masterpieces. And I kept trying to conjure up my last image of you: standing there, frowning at me when behind you loomed your gang of

121

vicious inadequates. For there was the proof you weren't worthy of me. You were just too immature, for a start. That's what I kept telling myself. And then I thought of the knifing and how I couldn't help feeling involved in it. And guilty. No, that night was more than I could bear. I had to finish with you for my own sake.

But instead, all I did was give myself headaches. In fact, I got so many headaches my parents arranged for me to spend the last week of the holiday at my nan's in Scotland. They knew we'd split up and I didn't want to talk to you, so they figured out of sight, out of mind, I guess.

Then, the night before I left I went for a quiet drink with Debbie. (You met her once. She liked you.) But only seconds after I'd arrived in the pub I turned round and there you were. Jason, if you'd meant nothing to me I could so easily have faked a smile. Instead – but blanking you out was infantile. I guess I wanted to punish you. I don't know. I was scared, too. For you just wouldn't disappear from my life.

Afterwards I made one last desperate attempt to finish with you. That letter joined its ancestors at almost exactly the time you started writing to me.

By the time you posted your letter in my letter box I was beginning my journey to the Highlands. So I never saw your letter on Sunday and in fact it was only when my mum rang me on Monday night that she mentioned a letter had been hand-delivered and she thought it was from you. She nearly didn't tell me.

So, while you were wondering why I'd never replied to your beautiful letter I was deep in the Highlands, being fussed over by my nan who acted as if I was convalescing from a serious illness.

WHAT AM I DOING HERE JASON?

Coming here was my escape hatch. I saw myself walking the Highlands, rebuilding my life without you.

Only there's nothing here but emptiness. WITHOUT YOU.

So what are you doing now? Not thinking too badly of me, I hope. You do understand why I haven't written before this, don't you? There is one more thing I wanted to say. I do hope your gang is completely disbanded now. Not because I don't want you to have friends. I despise clingy, possessive girls and I'd like you to have lots of (male) friends. But if you go on in that gang, well, there'll just be more trouble. I'm right, aren't I? And you'll end up in prison, or dead.

I even dreamt I saw you lying dead in the gutter one night. The rain was beating down on you and you were calling out my name – so you can't have been quite dead – but I couldn't move, even my face was frozen. And then you called my name again, really urgently. This time I could run to you but it was as if I were running in quicksand and when I finally reached you, it was too late. The rain had washed you all away.

Still, they say if you dream something, the oppossite always happens. I hope so.

I want to see you so badly. But I'm exiled here until Saturday, after which I'm being driven back to school. If I can get home before then without totally annihilating my nan's feelings I definitely *will*. Meanwhile, she hasn't even got a phone. *I've never felt more cut-off.* That's why I must close this letter, to make certain I catch the day's only post.

Up here, I've realised one thing, Jason. I can't finish letters where I say goodbye to you. I'll never say goodbye to you.

Take care, o *totally* unvaporised one. What a mess!

Kara
XXXX

P.S. My dad may not like your leather jacket – that's his problem – but I do. I've always liked it.

Stranger in my Mirror

It began with a present for Liz: a car. In this car Liz is about to take a bizarre journey to – where exactly?

Stranger in my Mirror

It was a total shock. Especially as I had the driving examiner everyone dreaded. The one who never smiled and practically never passed anyone. But today, he'd done both and chatted to me about his daughter afterwards. Miracle followed miracle.

The following evening Dad was very late. But Mum didn't say, 'I wonder what's keeping your father?' and look up every time a car went by. And when he finally arrived they exchanged a smile usually reserved for birthdays.

'Little surprise for you outside, Liz,' said Dad.

It was the rarest kind of blue; just occasionally in the evening you might glimpse the sky turning that deep rich blue. But only after a perfect summer's day. I'd never seen a more beautiful Fiesta. And it was mine.

'We should have bought you a car long before this,' said Dad guiltily.

'Oh, no, you shouldn't,' I said. 'And you can't afford this.'

'Of course we can,' he said. 'Anyway, I managed to knock the price down quite a bit. I was surprised as it's hardly been used. Got a real bargain there, I reckon.'

I stood admiring the car for a long time. Too long.

'Well, aren't you going to take it for a spin?' Dad asked.

I shuddered. Passing my test had been one of those freaks of nature you read about. But I wasn't a driver. Hadn't my instructor said I still couldn't read the road? Still, such a glorious present must be unwrapped.

I edged inside. Pictures were taken. Then I waited for Dad to sit beside me.

'You don't need me now,' he said. 'Now's when you'll really start learning.'

Mum gave a small gasp as he said this. Dad frowned at her but even he added, 'Just go to the garage and back.'

They ran down the road, waving me off as if I were taking part in a major rally. At the top of the road I purped the horn. Twice. I'd always wanted to do that. A woman came out of her house. I vaguely knew her. I purped my horn again just so she'd know – so everyone would know – I was free. I could travel wherever I wanted to now, just provided it didn't involve too many roundabouts. Or right-hand turns.

I filled my car up like a veteran. Then I bought myself some chocolate in this little kiosk next to the garage. I can spend hours deciding what to buy and today I also had to consider whether my parents would prefer chocolate or mints. I was still deciding when I remembered something. I hadn't locked my car.

I rushed out of the kiosk. My car gleamed back at me. I nearly hugged it with relief. Imagine if I'd had it stolen after – I looked at my watch – nine and a half minutes' possession! It seemed rather tame just to go back home. So I decided I'd drive on a little longer, a little faster. All at once I was doing fifty. Fields sped by. I wasn't sure where I was going. I was just enjoying the sensation of feeling carefree, yet in control of things, too. For I could turn back whenever I wanted.

A junction loomed up. Which way to go? I looked into my mirror and saw a face staring back at me. A boy, about sixteen, was sitting at the back of my car, staring right at me. He must have jumped in while I was buying the chocolate. And he didn't seem the least bit bothered I'd noticed him. So he must have a gun or a knife.

In my haste to stop the car I stalled it, jolting myself forward. Then I leapt out and ran for my life. Never even in my worst nightmare, have I run so fast. Only then I never actually get anywhere while the horror draws closer and closer. But tonight – was he gaining on me? It was difficult to tell for my heart was thumping so loudly I couldn't hear anything else.

And now – where was I? Somewhere with no wind, no clouds, no life at all, just stillness. Even the trees seemed like models, carved out of the darkness.

I stopped and listened intently. Somewhere in this black fog could I hear muffled breathing? Would a shadow spring out at me? But nothing stirred. And then I realised it wasn't me he wanted but my car. So I'd done exactly what he wanted. He'd have turned round and driven far, far away in my beautiful car by now, leaving me to stumble further and further into this black hole.

Back up the road, about half a mile from where I stopped was a pub. I could go in there, beg 10p for the phone, ring my parents and oh, the shame of it. But I had no alternative.

I ran back the way I'd come, never expecting to see my car again. And certainly not for it to be exactly as I'd left it, with even the door still hanging open. Had he not been able to start the car? Was he still lurking in the back somewhere? I peered into the car but not for very long. Then I got in and locked the doors. Now I knew what had happened. I'd done it again, hadn't I?

How often had I woken up to feel someone's hot breath on my neck? How often had I seen someone sitting in the chair at the end of my bedroom? How often? Far too often. All my life strange misty figures had managed to crawl out of my mind and for a second actually appear, exist. I used to think there were little holes in the air which they crept in and out of. And even when I couldn't see them I knew they were there, hiding, ready to materialise suddenly when I was least expecting them. And there was nothing I could do. No one could. For no one had any power over them except . . .

'Next time you see them, just think as hard as you can of me,' my nan said. 'Picture me there in the room with you.' And I did. I pictured myself in earlier days, snuggling down beside Nan in her double bed, smelling her lavender scent, sucking one of her boiled sweets and listening to another story about my dad when he was a boy, and feeling totally happy and safe.

She was my eternal refuge. If, for example, my dad got mad at me – and occasionally he did – she'd immediately put her arm around me and say, 'Leave her alone, Tony, the world will knock her about soon enough.' And Dad's anger dissolved as swiftly by day as those phantoms did at night. Nothing could threaten my nan. As long as I could conjure her up I was safe.

Until the last time I saw her. It was a beautiful summer's afternoon and, even though the curtains were tightly drawn, a golden haze still hung over my nan like a supernatural wreath. And by the foot of her bed stood a small procession of us, all bearing flowers. Never had my nan's room been so ablaze with flowers, especially white carnations. 'These are her favourites,' people said reverently. But what use was that now? She couldn't smell them. She couldn't see them.

All morning I'd been crying, begging to be allowed to see her. But now I couldn't look at her. Even though people tried to tell me she was only sleeping. But I'd seen her sleeping before, many times. This wasn't sleeping. Just as she wasn't my nan any more. She was just a corpse. Last week I'd hugged her hard, today I couldn't bear to touch her. She'd joined the enemy. The night-time phantoms could strike wherever they liked now. And tonight they had a fresh victory. They'd invaded my new car. And that face would surely return regularly. Only next time I wouldn't let him scare me. He wasn't actually scary at all, just a boy really. Next time I must just square up to him and tell him to leave me alone.

Even so, I didn't drive the car for the next few days. But then I figured I was being cowardly and feeble and besides my parents were getting anxious. ('Don't you like your car?') So I drove over to my friend Angela's for a meal and a gossip. I hadn't seen her for ages as she lives so far out (although only half an hour in the car). And it was wonderful not having to phone up my dad for a lift and being able to stay with her for as long as I wanted. I even enjoyed the drive back home. For this time the sky was covered in tiny specks of light. I looked up at the stars and then I saw him again. He appeared in my mirror, just like before. For a moment there I nearly swerved the car but then my fear exploded into anger.

'Go away,' I yelled. 'Go away,' but even before I finished yelling he'd gone. He'd only appeared for a split second but long enough for me to realise I knew him. Or rather I'd seen him before. I was sure I had.

He had dark curly hair and was tanned and his eyes – he had very nice eyes. He was really quite good-looking, in fact. Was that why I'd remembered him? I'd definitely seen him but I'd totally forgotten where. The whole thing was very strange but not scary. After all, sinister phantoms weren't jumping out of my mind now, attractive boys were. A definite improvement. I smiled. If only I could remember who he was.

The following night it was bucketing down with rain and I was wondering how windscreen wipers could be both so ugly and graceful at the same time when I saw him for the third time.

Only this time he stretched his hand out to me and I heard him speak. He whispered, 'Anne,' and he seemed to say it right inside my ear. And for a moment I could hear a strange rushing sound, too, just as if someone had put a shell up to my ear. But then there was just the sound of the windscreen wipers again and cars hissing past me.

I lay awake thinking about him. All my phantoms had been misty-looking but he had seemed so clear, so definite, so real. And I'd never had a phantom speak to me before. I finally closed my eyes and slipped down into my worst nightmare, again. My nan has her arm around me and is stroking my hair. I'm lying beside her feeling so safe and content. I look up at her but there is nothing left except a skull. I scream and run to the door. Only this time the dream goes on. For he is standing at the door. His face staring at me just like in my car. And then he smiles, a bewitching smile that stirs my heart. 'Where have I seen you before?' I cry, stepping forward. But his face starts withering away, like my nan's. 'Oh, no,' I cry. 'Not you, too.' But he's gone. Only his skull remains.

As soon as I wake up I switch on every light in my bedroom but it's still not light enough. And I'm shaking like crazy. For now I know where I've seen him before. Or I think I do. He was on the front page of our local paper, five or six weeks ago. And he'd been in a car accident, hadn't he?

Early next morning in the library I read the full story: Sarah Payne, 19, and her boyfriend Michael Kemp, 17, had been returning home from a night out in London when Sarah's car was involved in a head-on collision with a van. The driver of the van and Sarah, who'd been driving her car, got away with cuts and bruises but Michael died on arrival at hospital. There were comments about him from his form teacher and his father (his mother was too upset to speak). 'He was a boy everyone liked,' concluded his form teacher. 'He was also one of the sixth form's most promising sportsmen.'

And there he was, grinning away, confident, brimming with life. I sat staring at his picture for so long, it actually seemed to start fading, just like the picture on my aunt's sideboard of my nan with her arm around me did. Every time I looked at it Nan seemed a little fainter, a little more ghost-like. In the end I was afraid to look at it just in case she wasn't there any more.

All day I walked round town choked with sadness. I was missing someone I'd never met, which was pretty absurd really. Still . . . I'd made one mistake. His girlfriend was called Sarah. I didn't know where I'd got Anne from. In a way that mistake reassured me.

I arrived home very late. My mum was not pleased. 'No point in me cooking you food if you're not going to come in until it's cold.'

'Can't we heat it up?' I said. I didn't want my mum to have a go at me. Not now.

But then my mum said, 'There's a very strange message for you on the answering machine. Was it one of your friends messing about?'

I dashed to the machine and played back tonight's messages. First there was someone from Dad's club. He went on for ages, then I heard, 'Liz Morgan, if you've been having disturbances in your new car recently, ring Anne Collins on . . .' *Anne*, the name I'd heard him call.

'Is that one of your friends? Do you recognise the voice?' Mum was beside me.

I didn't answer at first, just sat there in stunned silence. Then I said, 'No, it isn't one of my friends, Mum. I'd better ring her.'

'But what does she mean "disturbances"?', asked Mum.

I didn't answer. I was already dialling Anne Collins' number. Nobody answered the phone for ages and I was just about to put it down when I heard a woman's voice, breathless, suspicious. 'Yes?'

'May I speak to Anne Collins, please?'

'You've just missed her. I'm her mother. Who is this?'

'I'm Liz Morgan. I was left a message to contact Anne Collins. You don't know when she'll be back?'

'I've no idea.' She paused, then, 'Liz Morgan. She's mentioned your name.' A ripple of fear went through me. 'You're from this Spiritualist Centre down Fraser Street, aren't you?'

I shivered. 'Is that where she's going now?'

'Yes, I told her it wouldn't help and she's just going to get herself all upset again but she had to go, wouldn't listen to me.' Her voice suddenly switched. 'So I'm sorry, I don't know when she'll be back.'

I just told Mum Anne Collins was out.

'Sounds like a very silly practical joke to me,' said Mum.

I pretended to agree with her, then said I had to pop out for a while.

Outside my car sparkled and shone. It always reminded me of those days when you wake up to find the sun streaming through the window and the air so light and fresh you can't believe anything bad can happen. Just as you'd never believe my car could be haunted. But it could be.

I drove a little way, then stopped beneath a huge street light.

'All right, ghost,' I said, 'come on, produce yourself.' But it was only in my mind I saw his face, so full of life, so good-looking. 'Please, Michael, I want to help you.' But again, just a deafening silence.

I drove on to the Spiritualist Centre. And as I approached I felt a strange tingling sensation up and down my arms. And I heard, not a voice, but a noise like the soft swish of the sea. Or was it someone sighing? Was

134

it Michael? I kept looking over my shoulder. I wanted to see Michael now but the back seat was always empty.

I turned into the road, full of fat houses which smirked contemptuously at me. But the Spiritualist Centre was a lovely, three-storey 1920s house with a wonderful, wide staircase, high ceilings and all sorts of fascinating nooks and crannies. The sort of house I'd always dreamed of living in. Some of my apprehension left me. I was met in the hall by a guy in thick glasses. I went to get out my purse.

'No, there's no charge tonight,' he said, then he added confidingly, 'You're just in time.'

Our footsteps echoed on the wooden floor as he directed me into a room where a group of mainly elderly people were sat in a circle.

'If you don't feel that it fits, don't say that it does. "Test the spirits carefully": St Paul.' The woman talking stopped, smiled me into a large brown chair and whispered, 'You're very welcome.'

She was about forty-five, plumpish, office-smart, her hair held back in a rather severe bun but there was a watery dreaminess in her eyes and her lips kept thickening into smiles. She spoke in a low, soothing voice, too. She would have made a wonderful hypnotist.

'Now, I'm going to ask you to concentrate hard on your loved ones who are waiting to contact you . . .'

There was total silence, save for a cistern rumbling above us. I looked around for Anne. All heads were bowed except one. Was this her? She had blonde hair hanging loosely around her shoulders and would have looked most attractive if her face hadn't seemed to be drained of all colour. And her eyes – there was a blankness in her eyes that alarmed me.

Then the medium said, 'Remember the spirit people arrive on the wings of love.' Then she started talking to the air. 'Yes, Yes, all right, I know you are anxious to begin.'

Spirit people, what an odd phrase. It made the dead sound like leprechauns; the little people, the spirit people. No, that wasn't right, was it? Spirits weren't really massing around this room, were they – or were they?

I shivered. Was a new power surging through this room?

Then the medium said, 'I have someone here, spirit-side.' Everyone leaned forward except Anne. 'Someone who is very anxious to make contact.' Was it Michael or my nan? It might even be her. Did I want it to be? I half did and yet, I was scared too. . .

'Who is trying to contact someone called Florence?' the medium went on.

A frail hand was raised. 'I'm Florence,' she said.

'And do you have someone spirit-side called Ena?'

'Edie, my sister,' she corrected.

'Edie, yes, that's right,' said the medium.

Edie had happy messages for everyone in Florence's family. While Florence kept saying, 'That's right. Thank you. Oh, thank you.'

Then the medium said, 'And now I have someone who passed over spirit-side only recently, so he's not very clear yet . . .' She seemed to be straining her eyes to see him. 'He's just a boy, about sixteen.'

I let out a short cry.

'And he's saying, "My neck, my neck, I hurt my neck. Oh, it was a terrible accident."'

I wrapped my arms tightly around myself.

'And he's standing by you.' She was staring at the girl I'd identified as Anne. I waited for Anne to react but her face was expressionless. 'He says he loves you very much.'

Anne still didn't show any emotion. It was as if she was in a trance of her own.

136

The medium turned away from us and started behaving as if someone were pulling at her and becoming very agitated.

'Yes, yes, all right. I'll tell her, Michael. I promise.' Then, to no one in particular, she said, 'Poor boy, he's very agitated.' I strained my eyes. If only I could see Michael now, too. But I couldn't.

She turned to Anne. 'He's asking you to forgive him.' For the first time Anne lowered her face. 'He's begging you to forgive him.'

At this Anne suddenly shot up. 'Forgive him! I'll never forgive him. Will you tell him that? I'll never forgive him.'

'You must forgive him now,' murmured the medium. 'For the weight of all that bitterness . . .'

'I can't. I can't.' Her voice fell away and she sped from the room. Immediately I ran after her.

In the hallway she whirled round. 'What do you want?' she said.

'I'm Liz Morgan,' I said. 'You left a message for me today. Your mum said you were here.' My words went echoing round and round the hall and I felt as if I were in one of those dreams you have when you're just on the borders of sleep. Any moment I felt this scene between Anne and me would just dissolve away.

'You've had disturbances in your car, haven't you?' she asked.

'Yes, I have.'

She moved closer to me. 'That car was mine. I sold it because of those – those disturbances. But then I felt guilty. I thought, if something suddenly happened to you, you might crash the car. Did you hear strange whispering noises?'

I nodded. 'And I saw him.'

'You saw him, too?'

'The first night I drove the car I saw him in my mirror. I

saw him two other times and once I heard him call your name.'

'You heard him call me?' She faltered for a moment. 'But it's too late now. Too late. Just why did he do it?' she demanded suddenly. 'We'd been going out together for almost a year, you know. He was my whole life. So when I heard he'd been killed in a car crash . . .' She faltered again. I went to put my arms around her shoulder.

'No, I'm all right,' she said, recovering herself. 'But when I heard he'd been with her and been seeing her behind my back for two months, well, it was as if he died twice. Only the second time he shattered not only our present and our future but our past, too. He's left me with *nothing*.

'And I'd drive my car – before, I'd called it our car because we'd gone everywhere together in it – and know he was still there. He wanted to contact me but what was the point? He'd destroyed everything between us. So I told my dad the car had too many memories, which was true, and he sold it.

'But then I thought, if he wants to contact me, well, let him – so I can tell him why I'll never forgive him. And I can't forgive him. Anything else I could have. Even if he'd murdered someone I'd have stood by him. But to lie and deceive me for all that time when I – well, why shouldn't he suffer, too? You don't blame me, do you?'

I looked at her face, a tight mask of pain. 'No,' I said, 'I don't blame you.'

We stood outside together, the sky blotchy and stained with rain.

'I must go,' she said.

It was then I saw Michael. He was standing beside my car and beckoning. At first I thought he was beckoning to me but it was Anne he was staring at.

'Look, look,' I exclaimed. 'By my car. Can you see?'

'No, no, I can't,' cried Anne, turning her face away.

For a moment I thought Michael was going to move towards us. But he didn't. He just stood there, gazing over at Anne.

'Anne, please look.' I was gasping, for seeing Michael again like that seemed to catch me by the throat. 'Anne,' I began again but it was too late. There was just the rain drizzling down on my car.

'He's gone,' I said flatly.

But Anne still didn't turn round. And I think I understood why. She'd wound up so much hurt inside her she was afraid to let it go. But in the end that was exactly what she had to do. It seemed so trite to say something like that to her. Yet, what else could I say? I've never loved a boy as much as her.

I felt sorry for them both. But what good was that? I had to do something and quickly. Anne was going. It was then I had an idea. 'Anne, you won't mind if I sell the car tomorrow, will you?'

She started. 'Sell it.'

'Yes. I don't want a haunted car so I'll get my dad to sell it tomorrow. So if you know of anyone who wants a car and likes ghosts, tell them to call at 10 Daltons Close, will you?'

'Yes, yes, all right,' said Anne slowly. A tiny light formed in her eyes, like the glimmer of sunlight on the surface of a lake.

I gushed on. 'Because the sooner I sell this car now the better I'll feel.' Then, because I always have to overdo things, I added, 'So, with a bit of luck, you'll never see this car again.'

At this she actually flinched. And I feared I'd gone too far. I'd wanted to give Anne a jolt, not a body-blow.

Next morning my mum burst into my bedroom. 'Liz, I think your car's been stolen.'

I shot out of bed, then I remembered and smiled.

139

'Don't worry, Mum,' I said. 'I think this car has been borrowed by a friend – two friends – of mine.'

And later, under all the junk mail I found a note: 'Dear Liz, I had to borrow your car before you sell it. I hope you don't mind but it's urgent. Anne.'

At lunchtime Anne and car returned. We spent the afternoon together and even phoned the Spiritualist Centre where we spoke to the medium. Then Anne left, this time hugging me before she went and I took the car out, just to check . . .

But Anne was right. Nothing but a gaping emptiness was in my car now. Yet earlier this morning, when Anne had borrowed my car (I'd left it unlocked), she saw him, smiling at her in the mirror. And even without her saying a word he knew she'd forgiven him. And then she felt something, like a summer breeze passing over her; he left as silently and as swiftly as a light going out.

'He's free at last. Now he has other dreams to dream. You both have,' said the medium.

And there were tears in Anne's eyes as she said, 'I've lost him, yet I've got him back, too.'

Now there are tears in my eyes and not just for Anne. I never even got the chance to say goodbye to Michael. And now my secret passage to him has been walled up. I'll never see him again. And I'd give anything to see him just once more.

And that night I did. Suddenly, there he was in my dream. He was standing in this meadow. And he was beckoning to me. *To me.* I rushed over but as soon as I reached him he'd vanished. I looked down and saw what he'd been pointing at: my nan lying asleep on the grass, just as I'd seen her at a picnic years ago. She even had that same picnic hamper beside her.

I stood a little way from her, calling and calling, but she never woke up. Finally, I crept nearer, ready to jump away when her head turned into a hideous skull. But this time it was as if I were seeing her face in a giant close-up. And I could see that she was smiling. She must have been having such a beautiful dream. I drew closer. I could even smell her lavender perfume. Suddenly I bent over and I kissed her gently on the lips. Then, even though I knew she could never wake, I tiptoed quietly away.

Denis Bond

ROUGH MIX

Two teenagers – Terry Smith and Ray Rosetti – want desperately to be pop singers. But that's *all* they have in common.

Terry, a gypsy, is a loner, never part of the crowd. Rosetti is rich, good-looking and confident. Backed by his father's money Rosetti is able to form and front his own group: they're talentless but well-packaged.

Terry *is* talented, and with help from a teacher signs with a small, independent record label. But as success becomes the most important thing in his life, a tragic event and its consequences force him to re-examine his new career. He faces an impossible choice – either to fulfil his ambition or to remain loyal to his family . . .

Mary Hooper

CASSIE

Cassie's one wish is to be a journalist, in a trench coat, carrying a reporter's note book, hot on the trail . . .

So when she gets a job as Junior on the Weekly Echo her dream comes true, or does it? Making endless cups of coffee, columns of supermarket bargains. Not *another* hundredth birthday!

But then there's always Gavin, the dashing photographer from *Sixteen-On*, or Simon, who's never far from Cassie's side.

A selected list of title available from Teens · Mandarin

While every effort is made to keep prices low, it is sometimes necessary to increase prices at short notice. Mandarin Paperbacks reserves the right to show new retail prices on covers which may differ from those previously advertised in the text or elsewhere.

The prices shown below were correct at the time of going to press.

☐	7497 0009 2	**The Secret Diary of Adrian Mole Aged 13¾**	Sue Townsend	£2.50
☐	7497 0101 3	**The Growing Pains of Adrian Mole**	Sue Townsend	£2.50
☐	7497 0018 1	**Behind the Bike Sheds**	Jan Needle	£2.25
☐	416 10352 9	**Lexie**	Mary Hooper	£1.99
☐	416 08282 3	**After Thursday**	Jean Ure	£1.99
☐	416 10192 5	**A Tale of Time City**	Diana Wynne-Jones	£1.99
☐	416 07442 1	**Howl's Moving Castle**	Diana Wynne-Jones	£1.95
☐	416 08822 8	**The Changeover**	Margaret Mahy	£1.95
☐	416 13102 6	**Frankie's Story**	Catherine Sefton	£1.99
☐	416 11962 X	**Teens Book of Love Stories**	Miriam Hodgeson	£1.95
☐	416 12022 9	**Picture Me Falling In Love**	June Foley	£1.99
☐	416 12612 X	**All the Fun of the Fair**	Anthony Masters	£2.25
☐	416 13862 4	**Rough Mix**	Denis Bond	£1.99
☐	416 08082 0	**Teenagers Handbook**	Murphy/Grime	£1.99

All these books are available at your bookshop or newsagent, or can be ordered direct from the publisher. Just tick the titles you want and fill in the form below.

Mandarin Paperbacks, Cash Sales Department, PO Box 11, Falmouth, Cornwall TR10 9EN.

Please send cheque or postal order, no currency, for purchase price quoted and allow the following for postage and packing:

UK   80p for the first book, 20p for each additional book ordered to a maximum charge of £2.00.

BFPO   80p for the first book, 20p for each additional book.

Overseas   £1.50 for the first book, £1.00 for the second and 30p for each additional book
including Eire   thereafter.

NAME (Block letters) ....

ADDRESS ....

....

....